The Elder Chronicles

Volume 9

Armageddon

By

Robyn Kelly

This story is fiction. The settings are imaginary. Any resemblance of the characters or places to actual persons or places is purely coincidental.

Table of Contents

Prologue

Chapter 1:   Promotion

Chapter 2:   Homeland Security

Chapter 3:   Surveillance

Chapter 4:   Watson Takes Flight

Chapter 5:   Playing by the Rules

Chapter 6:   War Games

Chapter 7:   Intelligence

Chapter 8:   Arms Depot

Chapter 9:   The Frigate

Chapter 10: A Warning

Chapter 11: The Frigate

Chapter 12: The Valley

Chapter 13: Naomi to the Rescue

Chapter 14: Homeland Security

Chapter 15: Launch

Chapter 16: Terrorists!

Epilogue

Prologue

It was the Human-Elder mutants that benefited most directly from the Presidential directive that prohibited harassment of Elders. They, obviously, lived among the humans. The Elders in the Valley had neither need nor desire to leave the Valley. They were safe and quite happy, if a little crowded.

The Elders were looking forward to Red Hawk's next installment of their history. Most were well aware of the sudden appearance of the FBI agent. But they had no real idea of where he had come from or why. The rumors that were circulating just didn't smell right. The Elders were certain that Red Hawk would tell them what was really going on.

The session was scheduled for early afternoon. The Elders started gathering at noon to get a good seat. By the designated starting time, the area at the entrance was completely full and there were Elders up on the top of the butte looking down from the balcony seats.

Red Hawk and White Wolf made their appearance right on cue. Red Hawk was again wearing her wrap-around dress. Her hair seemed to be more gray than red. It was still held in place by her beaded headband. She was still using the totem stick as a cane. White Wolf was still wearing his breechclout and a headband restraining his long black hair. This time, however, he was wearing a medicine bag about his neck.

White Wolf waited until Red Hawk was seated in front of the crowd, then he sat down just behind her. Red Hawk sat quietly with her eyes closed until the crowd quieted. Then she opened her eyes and began the most chilling story the Elders had ever heard.

"You are, of course, aware that Naomi and Serena managed to convince the President of the United States to issue an executive order that prohibited any member of the Executive Branch from arresting, holding or harassing any Elder. That is working quite well.

"Unfortunately, in doing so, they were required to severely punish the Secretary of Homeland Security, who refused to follow the directive. As an incentive to behave, the Deputy Secretary was invited to watch. What Naomi and Serena didn't realize at the time was that the two men were good friends, very good friends.

"The Deputy said nothing at the time, but he was determined to avenge the action taken against the Secretary. It took him quite a while to manage that. He very quietly started searching for information on the Elders. His search was hampered by the executive order; no one in Washington would talk about them. Slowly he expanded his search. Still getting nowhere, he became desperate.

"This is the story of just how desperate he became."

Chapter 1

Promotion

Tom Watson was an FBI agent. He had survived four years of college, and three years of law school, and the FBI Academy. He had even survived a few very boring assignments. He was now in the ultimate boring assignment. He was assigned to the Portland, Oregon, field office, running background checks.

Only Tom didn't really run. He sat at his desk and made phone calls. When he did get out of the office, he walked around various neighborhoods knocking on doors, asking very surprised people if they knew so-and-so and what kind of person he, or she, was. Sometimes he even sent fingerprint cards to the Washington office for verification.

In a word, Tom was bored to tears. At times, though, the tears were primarily caused by his feet. Despite his years, Tom was still in excellent condition; but hours of pounding the pavement caused his feet to ache severely. When he stayed in the office to spare his feet, his behind got too much exercise just from sitting in his chair and was soon rivaling his feet.

Tom was ready for some excitement. So, he welcomed a call from his old Academy bunkmate, Fred Winston.

"Hi, Fred," Tom answered. "What's new?"

"Well," Fred replied, "I've just spent the last three years back at the Barn working on some special investigations." He didn't mean to rub it in – much. But Tom's aching feet and rear were keeping time with Fred's words.

"I knew about that, Fred ," Tom said. "You told me all about it last year. Something has just happened to prompt this call. Fess up!"

"Okay," Fred agreed, "In my spare time at the Barn, I cozied up to a few of the clerks in personnel. My effort seems to have paid off."

"What marvelous assignment did you wangle for yourself this time?" Tom asked, with just a touch of envy.

"In another month," Fred announced gaily, "I will be leaving here for sunny southern California. I will be taking over the San Diego office in March as station chief."

Tom had greatly mixed emotions. He was, of course, happy for his friend. Fred loved the ocean and sailing and fishing; and a warm, sunny climate would be perfect for him. But, Tom's sense of misery was suddenly very markedly increased.

"I'm glad it worked out for you," was the best Tom could manage.

"That's not all I got," Fred added. "I wouldn't forget my old buddy. Haven't I always heard you complain about cold, damp weather?

"Yeah," Tom admitted, "I'm tired of Seattle, Portland and Chicago."

"Well," Fred asked, "how would like hot and dry for a change?"

"How hot and how dry?" Tom cautiously ventured.

"Tucson hot and dry," Fred said.

"That sounds great!" Tom erupted.

"Well," Fred drawled, "it's a small satellite office. Phoenix gets all the big stuff. But, I think, maybe, I managed a little icing on the cake." Fred was drawing this out as long as he could. He was enjoying every moment of tormenting his old buddy.

"You mean I won't be doing more background checks on the immigrants," Tom managed to get in.

"How about," Fred paused for effect, "Station Chief."

"What?" Tom exploded.

"You report there in a month." Fred said. "Think you can handle it?"

"Of course I can," Tom sputtered.

"You'll be getting your orders in a few days," Fred said. "Once you get settled in, why don't you take a few days off and come over to see me? Now, I've got to pack and get the car ready for the trip. See you soon, buddy."

Fred was gone and Tom just sat there in a trance. Fred did love to tease him, but he had never pulled a cruel joke. Tom was certain that he would receive his orders in a few days as Fred had promised.

When Tom did receive his orders, he found that he was indeed to report to the Tucson field office in March as the station chief. Then noted a strange note attached to the orders. He was, without fail, to stop *en route* at the Phoenix office for a special briefing. The briefing would only last an hour or so. Tom could not imagine what could be so important, and so brief.

It was a cold, damp day in March, when Tom packed his clothes, his few belongings and his current project into his well-maintained old Mustang convertible and headed down Interstate 5 toward Los Angeles. A rain cloud persisted in following him all the way to Chico. Then the sun broke through and things began to look up.

Tom stopped for the night at an inexpensive motel around Los Angeles. The next morning he was off bright and early, across the desert to Phoenix. The rain cloud stayed away so Tom put his top down and thoroughly enjoyed the gloriously dry warm weather.

It was a little after one o'clock when Tom pulled into the entrance of the FBI compound in Deer Valley and found a parking spot in the underground garage. He made his way into the main building, stopped at the information desk and showed the clerk his ID and a copy of his orders. He was directed to room 1015.

Tom walked down the hall and around the corner to room 1015. It looked like the entrance to a bank vault. A large steel door stood open, but the entrance was blocked by heavy wooden doors, tightly secured by a cipher lock. Tom rang the bell beside the door and waited. The wooden door cracked open and a voice from inside simply said, "ID?"

Tom again produced his orders and ID card. The door closed. It opened again in a few minutes and a young agent invited Tom inside.

"Pardon the inconvenience," the young agent said. "My name is, Bob. This is the Top Secret vault and we have to be sure you are properly cleared before allowing you in."

"Top Secret?" In all his days running background checks, Tom had never seen anything more highly classified than Confidential. This was really a step up. Tom had only two thoughts. 'Am I really cleared for Top Secret?' and 'What pertains to Tucson that is Top Secret?'

The room was filled with filing cabinets and chart cabinets. All of them were closed and locked. Bob guided Tom to a small office at one side of the room. There were no windows in the room. Bob invited Tom to have a seat at the single table and said he would return shortly. Tom sat.

A few minutes later, Bob reappeared with a folder in his hand. The folder was marked, Top Secret, Cosmic in large red letters. Bob sat down, placed the folder on the table and began a well rehearsed spiel.

"Having been recently promoted to Station Chief, you now come under the purview of a new DoJ regulation. This regulation requires that you be briefed on a very sensitive matter and that you sign a certification that you have read and understand the briefing material. After I have left the room, open the folder and remove the regulation and briefing card. Read both of them thoroughly. As soon as you are familiar with the content, sign the confirmation sheet. Then place the regulation and the briefing card back in the folder and leave it on the table. Leave the signed certification sheet on the table as well. Then press the button on the side of the table and I will return. Do not leave the room until I have returned. Do you understand what you are to do?"

"I think so," Tom said, "But what if I don't understand the material, or need further clarification.?"

"Put the materials back in the envelope," Bob said, "and press the button. When I return I will locate someone who has been previously briefed to assist you."

"And if I don't agree to sign the certification?" Tom liked to cover all the bases.

"In that case," Bob said matter-of-factly, "Your appointment as Chief of Station will be immediately rescinded and you will be assigned to another, less sensitive position. Your continued career in the FBI will be in jeopardy."

That was an eye-opener. Tom thanked Bob for his information, waited until he had retired from the room and closed the door. Then Tom opened the envelope and read the contents as directed.

Tom let out a low whistle as he read about the existence of Aliens on Earth. He took a few more minutes to digest the information and to appreciate the prohibitions and penalties. Then he put the materials backing the folder and sealed it. He now understood the real meaning of 'Top Secret' and why this material was so marked. Tom signed the confirmation sheet and pressed the button.

Bob returned and took charge of the envelop and confirmation sheet. He thanked Tom for coming in and bid him a good journey to Tucson.

Tom returned his car and made his way back to Interstate-10 and east to Tucson. He arrived at supper time, found a motel near the FBI office building. He unloaded his belongings into his motel room and settled in for a good night's sleep.

In the morning, Tom dressed for work in a dark suit and tie and drove down the street to the FBI field office. It was located beside a small college in an industrial area. A simple one-story building and a lot of parking. He could not imagine being put in charge of such an obsolete facility. This had to be where Fred's joke came in.

Tom pulled up to the building and walked inside. He showed his ID to the receptionist. She pointed down the hall to the present Chief's office. Tom walked down the hall and knocked at the open door.

"C'mon in!" said a friendly older voice from inside the office.

Tom obeyed and found himself across the desk from an older agent lounging in a comfortable desk chair. He was not wearing a coat or tie and his sleeves were rolled up. The nameplate on his desk said, "Jeff Harding".

"What can I do for you, son?" Jeff asked.

"My name is Tom Watson," Tom said. "I believe I'm your replacement."

"Well, I'll be darned," Jeff drawled. "I was wonderin' when they were goin' to get around to putting me out to pasture. Welcome to Tucson, Tom."

Chapter 2

Homeland Security

Alan Burke, the current Secretary of Homeland Security, always arrived at his office at nine o'clock in the morning. He was a short man in his early sixties, about 5'5", balding, with glasses. The weather was still cool, so he was wearing a sweater beneath his somewhat rumpled sport jacket.

Alan Burke was mad. Ever since he had watched a couple of little Aliens turn his boss and friend into a vegetable, he had been out for revenge. His anger had festered for so long now that it had grown beyond all bounds of reason. It was an obsession. In fact, Secretary Burke was so wrapped up in this obsession that he left much of the operation of Homeland Security to his deputy. With the exception of a few meetings with the President and some formal affairs, he concentrated solely on his problem.

He was also frustrated. Despite all his efforts to date, he had been completely unable to locate the Aliens' home base. How could he avenge his boss and exterminate this infestation if he couldn't even find them?

Today, he vowed, he would try a new approach, one that was sure to work. He flipped the switch on his intercom and asked his secretary to get the Director of the National Reconnaissance Office on the phone. The NRO was the office that directed the government's satellite reconnaissance program. Burke had a scathingly brilliant idea.

In a few minutes, Burke's phone rang.

"Good morning, James," Burke said. "Please give me a call back on the secure line." Then he hung up.

Burke unlocked a large desk drawer to his left, removed the large secure phone, set it on his desk and plugged it into a special outlet. In a few minutes it rang. Burke picked up the handset and said, "Go to secure mode." He pressed the secure mode button on his phone.

There were a few crackles and whistles, then the Director asked, "How do you read me?"

"Five-bye", Burke said, indicating clear reception.

"I'm also five-bye," the Director replied, "What can I do for you, Mr. Secretary?"

"I have a project in mind, James," Burke said. "Are your birds still regularly tracking over Russia?"

"Yes, they are," the Director responded.

"Then I suppose that they also over fly the US on the back side?" Burke asked.

"Of course," The Director was puzzled.

"How hard," Burke proposed, "would it be for you to turn the cameras on while they are over-flying the US?"

"Technically it would not be a problem," the Director replied, "But we are prohibited by law from photographing the US without specific authorization."

"I'm giving you that authorization right now," Burke said sharply. "I want a packet of every pass you make over the US from now on, with start and stop coordinates noted. Can you manage that? Priority basis."

"I think I would rather run it by my boss before we begin," the Director hedged.

"That will not be necessary," Burke insisted. "This project is strictly between you and me. Consider it 'eyes-only'. Have the packets delivered to your office immediately after each pass. Then send them to me by special messenger. That will ensure proper security control. I will extract the information I need and will destroy the packet. There will be no trace of it left.

"I will expect the first packet within 48 hours. Thank-you for your assistance, James. Good-bye." Burke hung up the phone before the Director had a chance to object further. For the first time in many moths Burke was actually smiling. He disconnected his phone and placed it back in the drawer.

The first packet arrived two days later by special messenger. In the meantime, Burke had a large drafting table set up in one corner of his office, complete with a bright lamp and a high-speed laptop capable of handling the new packet devices that had superceded the old DVD's.

Burke immediately powered up the laptop and inserted the packet into the reader. He noted the start coordinates and selected a corresponding map, which he spread out on the table. Then it was a simple process to compare the satellite image to the map and note any discrepancies.

So began the process. Every day, Burke would compare satellite imagery with known features from the latest maps. He hoped that, by sampling enough images, he would eventually come up with an anomaly that would indicate the Aliens' home. It was a long and random process, but it was the best he could come up with at the time. It gave him something to do and probably kept him from losing his mind completely.

For a while, the packets arrived on a daily basis. Burke was almost always at his table pouring over his maps. He felt, with some justification, that he could ignore cities and larger towns. According to what he had learned, the Aliens had been on Earth for over 1000 years. Certainly they would not have settled, or remained, in any built-up location. He believed that they had shunned human contact.

So Burke concentrated on the mountains and desolate spots around the country. If there was a large community of Aliens hidden somewhere, there had to be some visible evidence of it. And that evidence would most likely not be on a map.

A few months later, Burke had found nothing. He consoled himself with the thought that the satellites covered random areas of the country, depending on their requirements for covering Russia and other foreign locations. Sometimes, he even got virtually duplicate coverage of the US, causing further delays. But, still, he was doing something and that mattered the most.

About five months into the program, Burke received a call from the Director of the NRO asking for a call on the secure phone. Burke obliged him. After the usual preliminaries, Burke got an earful.

"I'm sorry, Mr. Secretary," the NRO Director said, "but, after the end of this week, the packet shipments will end. The satellite is being redirected and will no longer be covering the US at all. I hope you have enough material for your project by now."

Burke's response was not printable. By the time he had hung up the call and secured the phone, he was practically in panic mode. He had only covered about three-fourths of the desolate country. The amount left was huge. And only one or two more packets remained before the satellite changed orbits. Burke was determined to make the best of what he had left.

Burke concentrated very hard on the two remaining packets. The first one covered an area he had already plotted. But Burke went over it again, frame by frame. He could see nothing. The last packet arrived at the end of the week. It covered a new area of the western US. Again, Burke went over it frame by frame, plotting each frame on his map.

As the last frame came up on the computer screen, Burke was ready to just pack it in. His great hope had not panned out. Then he noticed a small anomaly in the bottom left corner of the frame. It was part of something larger. He couldn't quite make it out. He quickly searched his supply of maps for a 250-scale that covered this area.

Burke found the map and spread it out. He checked the coordinates from the larger map and located them on the 250-scale map. The area indicated looked to be a large butte. Burke looked again at the image. It only contained a portion of the butte. But the image didn't look like any butte he had ever seen.

Burke couldn't believe his luck. The last image on the last packet just might be what he had been looking for all along. But first he had to verify it. Then he had to determine the actual coordinates.

Burke put the '250' on his desk. He extracted the packet from the computer and put it along with the other marked up maps into a burn bag designated for classified destruction. He went back to his desk and told his secretary to have the weekend cleaning crew remove the drafting table and light.

He was about to call his investigators and have them pay a visit to … where? … Arizona, according to the map. Then he had a better idea. He told his secretary to connect him with the head of the FBI.

When the Director came on the line, Burke said,

"Good Afternoon, Director Williams, this is Alan Burke, Secretary of Homeland Security, I have a little favor to ask of you."

"Of course," the Director responded. "What can I do for you?"

"I would like one of your agents to physically check a certain set of coordinates and report what he finds there."

"Where are these coordinates?" the Director asked.

"Somewhere in Arizona, I believe," Burke answered. "Not too far from Tucson. I need the information as soon as possible." Burke read off the coordinates he had computed.

"I think I can accommodate you," the Director said. "Probably by the first of the week."

Burke thanked the Director and hung up the phone. He was, hopefully, only a few days away from the answer to his prayers. Burke left the office that evening happier than he had been in months.

Chapter 3

Surveillance

Director Williams thought long and hard about Secretary Burke's request. In his opinion, Burke had more than enough investigators on his staff, or within Homeland Security in general, to handle such a simple surveillance matter. 'Why did he want to involve the FBI?' the Director wondered. 'Was this, perchance, an FBI matter, having nothing to do with Homeland Security?'

Williams was more apt to think that this was something that Homeland Security didn't want to get involved with. 'Perhaps too political?' 'Perhaps too dangerous for some other reason.' He decided to sleep on the matter.

The next morning, Director Williams got a cup of coffee and sat down at his computer. He entered the coordinates into a map generator and stared at the results. He was staring down at what appeared to be the top of a butte. Nothing but desert all around. No, to the east was a two-lane road. It seemed to be a paved road. There was no traffic on the road. The Director looked at the shadows. There was a slight shadow to the east. The images were likely taken just after noon. Williams looked for the date of the images. Most of the images were dated 2032, two years ago.

'What,' he wondered, 'had happened in the last two years to make an on-site surveillance so necessary? An immigration problem? Not likely, this site was miles from the border and immigration was Homeland Security's province. Well, his time was running out. He had promised Burke that he would have an answer on Monday and he had to give his field agent some time to work with.' Williams closed the mapping program and yelled to his husband to call for his car. He needed to go into the office for a few hours. Then he went upstairs to get dressed.

When Williams got to the office, he told his driver to wait for him. He first stopped at his secretary's desk and looked up the number of the Tucson field office. When the Duty Officer answered, he said,

"This is Director Williams. Is the Chief of Station available?"

The Duty Officer almost inhaled her coffee, then sputtered, "He's not in the office at the moment sir. He can be here in about thirty minutes."

"Tell him to make it twenty," the Director said, "and to be ready to receive a secure call."

There was a click and the line went dead.

The DO immediately notified Tom of the call she had just received and encouraged him to get the office in fifteen minutes, even if that were impossible. She then went into the Chief's office and extracted the secure phone from the filing cabinet where it was stored and plugged it into the appropriate receptacle. She checked it to make sure it was operating properly and went back to her coffee cup to wait.

Almost precisely fifteen minutes later, the DO heard Tom's Mustang careening around the corner and skidding into his parking place in the lot outside the door. When he stepped in the door, he was a disheveled mess: hair totally wind blown, unshaven, shorts, t-shirt and sandals.

"Has he called back?" Tom gasped somewhat nervously, dropping into his desk chair.

"Not yet," the DO replied, not quite stifling a snicker.

"Well, the least you can do is pour me a cup of coffee," Tom suggested.

The DO complied. Tom took a sip, grimaced and said, "Good coffee, Sandy! Any idea what this is all about?"

"Not a clue, Boss" Sandy said and settled into a chair across from the desk.

At that moment the secure phone let out a wail. The two agents started and just stared at the phone. "You'd better answer it," Sandy suggested.

Tom suddenly woke up and grabbed the handset from the cradle.

"Tom Watson, Chief of Station," he said weakly.

"Good morning, Tom," the voice on the other end of the line replied. "This is Director Williams. How do you read me?"

"Five-bye," Tom said.

"Same here," The Director replied. "Are you alone?"

"No, sir," Tom said. "My DO is with me."

"With all apologies," the Director said, "Tell your DO to find something important to do elsewhere. What I have to say is for your ears only."

Tom complied. Sandy scowled briefly at Tom and exited the office, closing the door behind her.

"I am alone, now, sir," Tom announced.

"I have an assignment for you, Tom," the Director explained. "And for you alone. You are not to discuss this assignment with anyone, nor are you to involve anyone else. It is yours and yours alone. Do you understand?"

"Yes, sir," was Tom's only comment.

"You'll need a small piece of paper and a pencil. No pen!" the Director continued. "Write on a hard surface, no indentations. Now copy down these coordinates ... " The Director read off the coordinates and asked Tom to read them back to him. When he was satisfied that Tom had correctly written them, he continued, "You are to go to exactly these coordinates. You can use a simple GPS device to help you locate the spot, but don't use anything with a memory. There is to be no record that you ever knew about these coordinates or ever

24

visited the location. Once there you will photograph the exact spot from above and then take photos of everything around the spot for a distance of at least 100 yards. Take extra close-ups of anything interesting. When you return to the office, wrap up the camera as Top Secret information and express-ship it directly to me. My eyes only. Destroy the piece of paper and the GPS unit completely. You will never mention this assignment or what you may see at the coordinates to anyone. Do you understand?"

"Yes, sir, I do," Tom replied.

"I'm sending you on what could be a very dangerous assignment, Tom," the Director cautioned. "Both physically and career-wise. Be especially alert and careful. I look forward to receiving your report no later than Monday. Good-bye." The Phone went dead; the Director was gone.

Tom was stunned, and a little numb. Then he put both his mind and his feet in gear.

"Stow the phone, Sandy," he ordered as passed by her on his way to the door. "And tell George to take over for me if I am not back on Monday."

"What?!" Sandy called to Tom's back as he headed out the door to his car.

Tom's first stop was his apartment where he changed into more appropriate clothes. Then he stopped at a mall where he purchased a small GPS unit and a camera. When he got back to his car, he entered the coordinates the Director had given him into the GPS. He had absolutely no idea where they were. The GPS indicated that the target was in Arizona, about 60 miles north of Tucson. Tom headed out on the highway, following the route suggested by the GPS.

Tom made the extravagant decision to obey the speed limits, so it took almost 90 minutes to reach the little town of Winton. Tom stopped for fuel. While he was there, he recalibrated the GPS. It indicated that his route out of Winton was a little road that ran north through the Indian reservation.

Just at the edge of town, there was a big sign touting the new casino by Wakulla. Tom wondered if that was his destination. He drove slowly, constantly watching the GPS and comparing what it indicated to the landscape. His was virtually the only car on the road.

When he got to the turn-off for the casino, he lost the few cars that had been following him. He could see two buttes off to his left. The GPS seemed to be pointing in their direction. Tom slowed even more. The closer he came to the buttes, the more the GPS indicated the second butte. Tom looked at the ground to the left of the road. It was almost totally loose sand. There were a few small plants, a few cacti, but nothing significant.

Tom really did not want to just take off across the desert with his Mustang. It was designed to be a pretty muscle cart, not a cross country vehicle. Then, as he approached the larger of the two buttes, he noticed a well worn track leading to his left. He uttered a brief prayer and turned onto the track. The butte was only about two hundred yards from the road. It had steep, even sheer, bare sandstone walls about 60 feet tall. It appeared to be almost a mile long.

The GPS track indicated a spot on top of the butte, near its center. The closer Tom got, the more the GPS settled right on top on the large butte.

The track Tom was on led to a small opening in the south end of the butte. He wondered if this could be his destination. As he came abreast of the opening he could see that it was a short canyon. Just big enough for a cabin, a small corral and a few other small structures. The corral was empty and the GPS indicated that his goal was still almost half the length of the butte away. Maybe a thousand yards off.

Tom had no idea that he was in the middle of the tribe's sacred ground. He only knew he had an assignment to complete and he did not want to be interrupted in the process. He knew he was risking soft sand, but he continued on around the butte. He stayed near the butte where the ground was covered with pieces of shale that had fallen the wall. It was ruff, but better than getting stuck in loose sand. When Tom reached a point directly west of the GPS mark, he stopped.

Chapter 4

Watson Takes Flight

Tom Watson was at the base of the butte looking up. His goal was up there somewhere. It might just as well have been a million miles away. From his position, he could see no way to reach the top of the butte short of a helicopter; and he did not have a helicopter.

Tom decided that he really needed to check out the entire butte. Maybe there was a way up that he hadn't seen yet. He parked his car at the side of the butte. Then he started a fast jog around the base of the butte.

Tom did his best to stay on the shale deposits that had fallen from the wall of the butte. He had had a taste of running in sand while he was at the FBI Academy. He didn't especially like it. As he ran, he kept looking up at the top of the butte, hoping to find some way to access it from the ground.

It took about fifteen minutes to get back to the south end of the butte. Tom stopped there and looked again at the lower canyon walls. He guessed that they were only about forty feet high. But, even from the roof of the lean-to, he would need grappling hooks to reach the top. It wouldn't even be a sure thing from there.

Tom did a slow jog back to the car. Ever since he had discovered his goal, Tom had known what he needed to do. It was just that he didn't want to risk it. He opened the trunk of the car and stared at the contents. It looked like nothing more than a jumble of pipes and nylon and some extraneous equipment. It was Tom's latest off-duty project.

Tom liked to tinker. He was always working on some crazy idea. His latest project involved manned flight. Oh, yes, airplanes and helicopters had been around for ages. And they had been pretty much perfected. But neither was suited for surveillance. He knew that the military had been working on a way for men to fly without a vehicle, jet propelled backpacks and the like. They had even made some progress. Men could get off the ground and could fly some distance before they had to land again. But these devices were noisy and smelly. And they had yet to devise a way for someone to hover quietly.

That was Tom's challenge. How to give an agent the ability to hover silently and just watch a situation. Such an agent could provide intelligence, or call in the big guns, if they were necessary. Tom had almost succeeded. 'Almost' was the key word. His apparatus needed more testing. There were still a lot of little bugs to work out.

Tom began unpacking the car's trunk. The pipes and cloth he set aside. At the moment, he was interested in the backpack and the engines. He checked the remaining fuel supply: barely enough to get up to the top of the butte and back. It would have to do. First he fitted the propulsion arms into place in the engine's thruster vents. Then he slipped his arms into the upper straps of the back pack and pulled the lower straps between his legs, pulling them very tight. He shrugged a couple of times to ensure that the pack was properly positioned and the propulsion arms balanced.

Next came Tom's secret ingredient. The wing. Tom had cut down an old parachute wing and fastened it to two poles which he then inserted into holders on either side of the backpack. Once he was airborne, Tom could raise the wing and float quietly, use it to coast back to the ground, or lower it for some serious flying. Tom secured it in the lowered position.

The bait had been cut, now it was time to fish. Tom stepped away from the car, eyed his target position at the top of the butte and started the engine. He waited a moment to ensure that it was functioning correctly and applied power.

The little engine easily generated enough power to lift Tom off the ground and send him sailing upward toward the top of the butte. As he neared the top, Tom pulled out the GPS unit and his camera. He put the camera strap around his left wrist and held the GPS in his left hand. He used his right hand for the controls. He was a bit unbalanced, wobbling ever so little as he maneuvered the jets.

Tom reached the top of the butte and swiveled so that he could look in towards the center. He almost dropped the GPS. The whole butte appeared to be hollow. Not only that, but there was a pine tree forest growing inside it. Tom blinked several times. He could not believe his eyes. He checked the GPS. The spot he was looking for was toward the center of the butte. Tom started to move that way. He raised the wing and cut power way back. He began floating over the trees toward the center of the butte.

But the fates had other ideas for Tom that day. His engine coughed twice and died. Without the engine's help, the wing was totally incapable of keeping him aloft. Tom started to sink – rapidly – toward the floor of the butte. He found himself immediately surrounded by the trees.

The tree branches started tearing the flimsy wing to shreds. Tom was falling faster and faster toward the ground, bouncing off tree branches and doing his best to keep his legs together. (He had seen pictures of paratroops who come down straddling a tree branch. It wasn't pretty.) The last thing Tom remembered was being scared to death.

An Elder guard had seen Tom's car approaching the butte. She watched him park almost directly below her position. She followed him along the top rim as he ran around the butte. He was obviously looking for something and not finding it. The guard notified Mila, the nearest Council member, and continued watching. When Tom had donned the flying gear and taken off, the guard sent an emergency message to Mila and sped off the wall down into the Valley, in case her help was needed.

At the first alarm, all of the Elders quickly dispersed into the shelters. When Tom rose over the Valley, there was no one in sight. The Elders hoped that, seeing nothing in the butte, the stranger would just give up and go away. No one anticipated the crash. When Tom did crash, the Elders had another problem. The Councilors who had gathered in the Council chambers immediately took up the matter.

Arguments erupted on two sides. One side recommended escorting the stranger out of the Valley and erasing any memory of its existence from his mind. The other said, if they did that, he would only be back. They recommended finding out what brought him to the Valley in the first place and then deal with that. In the end, the Council decided to follow the second course of action.

After Tom's crash, a small group of Elders went to the site to see if he was still alive, and, if so, how badly he was hurt. They found Tom alive, but unconscious. His clothes had been torn up by the branches. He was bruised, but had no broken bones. His flying apparatus was scattered around him in shambles.

The Elders were not skilled in healing humans, but they knew enough to make Tom comfortable and to apply cold compresses.

For his part, Tom was quite groggy when he first woke up. He could barely make out some white forms hovering around him. His first thought was that he was dead and the images were angels. But, he reasoned, if he were really dead he surely wouldn't hurt so much. In a few more minutes, his vision cleared and he could make out the strange people clustered around him.

Tom tried to stand and ended up leaning back against the trunk of a tree. He slowly attempted to move, but still leaned heavily on the tree for support.

The Elders stood back and let him do what he could. About that time, Mila and two other Councilors arrived on the scene.

"How are you feeling?" Mila asked.

"Alive, and wishing I weren't?" Tom offered.

"Is there anything we can do to help you?" Mila asked, not really expecting any particular request.

"Where am I?" Tom asked. It had been a long time since he had seen 'The Wizard of Oz'.

Mila answered frankly, "You are in Arizona, in the center of a large butte that collapsed in upon itself ages ago."

Tom's head was beginning to clear. He looked around. Pale white humanoids about five feet tall, virtually hairless, black eyes. That briefing he had just had in Phoenix. These people were Elders! He was in the middle of Elder City! His head started to ache again as he contemplated the complications of his assignment.

"I really beg your pardon for dropping in on you like this," To began. "I assure you that I had no intention of bothering you." That sounded horrible. Tom tried again. "I mean I didn't know you were here; I wasn't really looking to find you. It was all just a big mistake. Oh, crap!" Tom gave up.

Mila was watching Tom carefully, noting not only what he said, but how he was saying it. "Don't worry," she said. "I believe you. But where do we go from here?"

Tom was getting his bearings. He stood up and took off the backpack. The camera was still attached to his left wrist. He put it in his pocket. He looked at the remainder of his flying gear. The propulsion arms were bent. They would not fly again without a lot of machining. The wing was in pieces, tiny pieces. One nozzle was missing entirely. Tom looked around and spotted it lay under another tree. Tom slowly walked over and picked it up and added it to the pile of junk.

Another look around and Tom asked, "Anyone seen my GPS unit? It's about so big." Tom used his hands to indicate about four inches.

In a few seconds, an Elder approached, holding out the GPS, "I believe this is it," she said.

Tom thanked her and put the GPS in his empty pocket.

"With your permission," Tom said to Mila, "I will be happy to leave this area right now. And I promise I will never return, or tell anyone what I have seen here." He looked around for some signal of agreement. For a moment or two nothing happened.

Mila looked at the mess on the ground beside Tom. "I take it," she said, "that your flying contraption is no longer capable of getting you safely over the rim of the butte to the ground."

"That is correct," Tom agreed, "I really hope that you have some sort of an exit from the butte that I can use."

"I think we can manage that," Mila said. Three Elders cam forward and picked up the parts of Tom's flying apparatus. "Pease follow me," Mila said. She turned and walked off toward the south end of the butte. The Elders with Tom's gear joined her. Tom started to follow meekly; then he had one of his few really brilliant ideas.

"Wait!" Tom called out. Mila stopped and looked back at him "There is one thing you could do for me," Tom said. "If you are willing," he hastily added. He knew he was risking the Elders' ire, but somehow he felt a few extra moments would be tolerated.

"What might that be?" Mila asked as she came back to Tom.

"I would like to take one picture before I go," Tom said. It did not take a genius in interplanetary relations to see that idea was not going to be received gladly. Again Tom hastily explained, "I don't want a picture of any of you or anything else in this butte." He reached in his pocket and pulled out the GPS unit. "I just want a close-up of this GPS unit sitting at zero and laying on the ground. If I can get that, I think I can keep other nosy people from bothering you again."

Mila was taken aback. She didn't quite know what to think or what to do.

"Let me set up the picture," Tom begged. "Then, if you don't want me to take it, I won't. I'll just go quietly."

Mila thought a bit longer. Then she said, "Show me."

Tom checked the GPS to ensure it was working and still set to the original coordinates. Everything seemed to be in order so he slowly started walking in the indicated direction. About ten feet away, the unit flashed and buzzed, indicating it was at the coordinates.

Tom stopped and looked around. He spotted a sandy patch of ground just a few feet from his position. Tom tried to remember his basic arithmetic: One second equaled about 100 feet. Piece of cake! Tom walked over to the bare spot, kneeled down and used the GPS device to make a flat, unmarked spot in the sand. He laid the device, still flashing, onto the sand and stood up.

Tom took out his camera and motioned for Mila to join him. "All I want to do," he said, "is to take a picture of that device from directly above. Is that okay?"

Mila looked at the GPS and asked, "Won't that show others the location of the Valley?"

"Not when I get through," Tom stated flatly. The rest of my pictures will show that GPS located out there in the dessert. My report will be entirely negative. No mention of you or the interior of the butte or anything."

"Besides," he added, "They already have these coordinates."

"Take your picture," Mila said. "Then you must leave."

Tom stood up next to the GPS device and moved close enough that his feet would be visible in the photograph. Then he took out the camera, adjusted the zoom to focus in the GPS and his toes and snapped the picture. He then picked up the GPS and put it and his camera into a pocket.

"Let's go," he said.

The little group left the shelter of the trees and crossed the open ground toward an obvious cave in the end of the butte. The three Elders with Tom's gear entered the cave. In a few minutes, they returned without the gear.

Mila turned to Tom. "I will take you through the cave," she instructed Tom. "You will find the interior without light of any kind. It will be a tight fit for a person of your size. There are several twists and turns. If you take the wrong turn at any point, you will never make it through to the outside. Hold my hand and do not let go. I will guide you."

Mila started into the cave and held out her hand. Tom took hold of it and held on. The cave was indeed dark. Tom quickly lost track of the twists and turns. In a few minutes, he followed Mila out of the cave and into the small canyon.

Tom saw his gear laying on the ground about ten feet away.

"Remember your promises to us," Mila said. She turned and reentered the cave, pulling a large bush over the entrance. Tom found himself standing in the canyon looking at a large bush with absolutely no idea why.

Tom turned around and found a tall, well built Indian, wearing a breechclout and headband, standing next to his gear. "Pick up your gear," the Indian said, "if you still want it, and follow me."

The Indian looked quite fit and his hand was resting on a knife hanging from his belt. Tom did as he was told. The two walked out of the canyon and to the right around the butte, until Tom's car was clearly in sight. The Indian stopped. "This area is sacred ground to my tribe. It is completely off limits to anyone who lacks permission from me to be here. You do not have my permission to be here. Return to your car, stow your gear and leave this area. Do not return."

Tom got the message.

Chapter 5

Playing by the Rules

Tom picked up his gear and lugged it back to where he had left his car. When he got there, he found that he had company.

There was an old beat up Jeep parked next to his car. Resting in the Jeep was a tall, older man dressed in a plaid shirt and jeans with a cowboy hat covering his face. As Tom got closer he noticed a blue light mounted on the Jeep just over what appeared to be an old .30-caliber carbine. As Tom reached his car, the figure came to life.

"I understand you dropped in on us by mistake," he said as he rose and stepped out of the Jeep. As the man turned to face Tom, he could see a star pinned to his shirt pocket and an old revolver hanging from his belt.

"Yeah, in more ways than one," Tom answered as he dropped his load on the ground behind his car. "Uh, just who might you be?" Tom did his best to sound more inquisitive than accusative.

"My name is Billy Eagle," the man said. "I'm the reservation sheriff. My job is to enforce the laws of my tribe."

Tom took due note of the type of laws Billy enforced. He opened the trunk and stowed his gear inside. It took a little cramming because of the bent pieces, but he managed. Then he closed the trunk and walked around his car toward the sheriff.

"I've just got one more task to tend to, then I'm out of here."

"What sort of task?" Billy had been lounging against the Jeep. Now he stood up in a more threatening posture.

"I have to take some pictures," Tom said, then hastily added, "nothing incriminating – I want to prove that 'they' don't exist." He nodded toward the Butte.

Then Tom had another brilliant idea. "How about just leaning against your Jeep and watching me," Tom suggested.

Billy didn't mind the 'watch' part, so he complied, ever ready to leap into action if events dictated.

Tom walked a few paces away from his car to a bare patch of sand. He took the GPS out of his pocket and looked at it. It was no longer flashing. He could compensate for that. He used the GPS device to smooth out the patch of sand then placed the unit in the middle of the patch.

Tom took care to make footprints in the sand by the GPS. Then he backed up a ways squatted down and started taking pictures. He put the GPS device in the bottom of the frame each time he took a picture, He moved around the GPS taking a picture every 45 degrees. He also made sure that two of his pictures included Sheriff Billy.

When he was through with his pictures he picked up the GPS device and headed to his car. As he started up the Mustang, Tom called over to the Sheriff, "How about leading me back to solid ground? I don't have four-wheel drive." The Sheriff obliged and Tom was soon back on the highway, headed to Tucson.

Tom took his time driving back to Tucson. He wanted to think about what needed to be done next. The Director wanted the camera. He had not asked for a report. Tom decided that he would include a brief report.

Tom was still having difficulty processing his first meeting with real aliens. When he read the briefing card in Phoenix, Tom had a 'yeah, sure' attitude about the Elders. Like most citizens, he had a really hard time accepting the fact that there were real, live aliens roaming around the universe, let alone existing right here in the US.

Now, he had just spoken to a real, live alien. He had seen at least a dozen of them. He was a changed man. Well, perhaps that was overstating it. But, he was torn at the moment. He would dearly loved to have had the chance to just talk with the Elders. How much they could teach him about life, about science, about religion!

But, he had sworn that he would do nothing to harass the Elders or to hinder them. Now, his Director, who had presumably read and sworn to follow the same guidelines, was asking him essentially to violate it.

Maybe not! Maybe the Director was simply replying to an outside request or an order from the DoJ. Maybe he did not know that the Elders were involved. Maybe.

Tom mulled over the possibilities. If he went one way, he would violate a sworn oath and subject himself to a severe penalty and/or punishment. If he went the other way, it could cost him his job. Tom liked the FBI and had invested a good chunk of his life into it. That would be hard to give up.

In the end, Tom decided that he would just play by the rules. Even if that wasn't the popular mode of life. He would discover if it was really better to honorable and honest.

But what to include in the report was problematical. He could never mention the Elders. His knowledge of them had to be limited to what was mentioned in the briefing sheet he had seen in Phoenix. He couldn't mention the coordinates; he was told to forget about them.

Tom framed the basic report in his mind and pulled a small voice recorder out of the center console.

"Re: Secure telecon with Director, FBI, 15 April 2034

Purchased small GPS device and digital camera.

Proceeded to location specified.

Met at location by Sheriff Billy Eagle, Reservation Sheriff.

Took requested photographs with digital camera.

Returned to office.

Comment: Location was immediately adjacent to large butte. There was no, repeat no indication of any items or subjects of interest at the location.

Will conclude assignment immediately upon return to office.

And that is just what Tom did. As soon as he got to the office he typed up his report, wrapped up the GPS device, the camera and the report according to the procedures for Top Secret material. Tom even threw in a receipt for the items in the package, but he really didn't expect to get that back. He put the Director's name, routing symbol and the words 'Eyes Only' on the inner wrapper. Then he put the FBI Headquarters address on the package and took it to a local FedEx office.

When Tom got home, he fixed a sandwich and a glass of wine for supper and immediately plunged his bruised and beaten body into a hot tub. Just out of habit, he checked his cell phone. There was a call from his girl friend , Rachael. He sent her a text saying he had a very bad day and would call her tomorrow. Then he just sipped his wine and soaked.

Tom's package arrived at FBI Headquarters early Monday morning. The mail clerk noted the general address on the outside and routed it automatically to bomb disposal. The bomb disposal people gingerly placed the package under a fluoroscope and discovered that the contents were harmless. They forwarded the package to Administration. By nine o'clock the package was on a clerk's desk. The clerk began unwrapping the package and saw the inner address and the Top Secret marking. She set the package aside and called for a cleared courier.

Director Williams had arrived at his desk and was enjoying a hot cup of coffee when his secretary notified him that a package had arrived marked Top Secret and for his eyes only. The Director marveled at the efficiency of his new Chief of Station in Tucson and asked his secretary to bring the package in.

When the secretary was leaving the office, Director Williams asked him to close the door. Then he pulled off the outer wrapping and noted the receipt as it fell out. He picked up the receipt, scanned it, scribbled something on it and set it in his out box. Then he shredded the inner wrapping and tossed it in his waste box. He observed the GPS, Tom's report and the camera. He first examined the GPS. It was still set to the original coordinates. The Director frowned. They should have been erased per his instructions. He set it aside for the moment

Next, the Director looked at the camera. He turned it on and checked for pictures. There were nine pictures in the memory. The Director scanned them in order. He was startled by the man standing by the Jeep. There was something in those photos. It wasn't immediately obvious; but it was there.

Director Williams picked up Tom's report and read it. Then he threw back his head and laughed so long and loud that he had tears in his eyes. The pictures were perfect, the report was perfect. He could not have expressed it better if he had tried.

When he had regained his composure, somewhat, he picked up the phone to his secretary.

"Tim," he said, "prepare a TS transfer for two miscellaneous items and tell my driver to meet me downstairs in ten minutes. I'm going over to DHS for about an hour."

The Director put his coat on and was contemplating what he would say to Alan Burke when Tim brought in the TS transfer. A quick trip down his private elevator to the garage and he was off to Homeland Security.

The Director's lapel pin and badge made getting through security a snap. He told his driver to wait. He anticipated a very short visit. He was soon in the Secretary's outer office waiting for an audience.

The Secretary came out to greet the Director and escort him into his office. The Secretary returned to his chair behind his desk. The Director remained standing in front of the desk. It was partly appropriate etiquette and partly wanting to be able to make a quick exit, should that become necessary.

"You have an answer for me?" Burke asked.

"I do," Williams responded. "I sent an agent out to examine the coordinates you gave me. He used this GPS device." Williams put the GPS unit on Burke's desk. Burke showed no real interest in it. "I told the agent to follow the GPS device to the coordinates and then to photograph the exact spot and an area around the spot for about 100 yards."

Burke, was beginning to salivate slightly. He really wanted to see those photos. Williams hesitated a little to let the desire grow. Then he pulled out the camera. "This is the camera he used," Williams said. "It has nine pictures on it. Those pictures indicate that he followed my orders completely. This is a copy of his report." Williams placed the report on Burke's desk and set the camera down on top of it. He kept his hand on the camera as he added, "He said he saw nothing of interest beyond what he photographed."

Williams released the camera and took a step back. Burke reached out greedily, like a child for candy and grabbed the camera. He turned it over and quickly scanned through the pictures. He looked at the camera as though he wanted more pictures. But there were none.

"What is this crap?!" the Secretary roared.

"Just exactly what you asked me for," Williams said quietly. "The Bureau is always happy to assist Homeland Security. If there is anything else we can do for you, don't hesitate to ask. You know we always play be the rules."

With that Director Williams turned and exited the office. There was a slight delay, then Secretary Burke stood up and hurled the camera as hard as he could across the room. It shattered against the far wall.

Chapter 6

War Games

Everything was going well at the Tucson FBI office. The Chief of the District had called Tom to tell him that the Director had put a glowing commendation in his file for the special assignment. Things were looking up. Things were also getting a little boring. A few skirmishes with illegal immigrants, a couple of AWOL sailors from San Diego, an incident at a bank that proved to be a false alarm: that was all Tom could manage for the past two months.

One fine day in June, Tom was lolling in his office. His coat was on the back of his chair, his tie loose, his shirt sleeves rolled up. He vaguely heard the phone ring in his secretary's office. Then his intercom interrupted his musings.

"Agent Winston from San Diego calling," she informed Tom.

Tom stopped musing and grabbed the phone.

"Hi, Buddy," Fred said. "Would you be free for a little vacation?"

"I'm always ready for a vacation," Tom replied. "I would really appreciate an exciting one."

"Not so exciting," Fred said, "but it should be interesting. We might even get in some deep water fishing."

"Tell me more," Tom perked up.

'The Navy is commissioning their new Frigate next weekend," Fred said. "It should be a good show and I have prime seating."

"That's it?" Tom knew his friend all too well. There had to be more for Fred to be so interested.

"Not quite," Fred teased. "The frigate is departing immediately after the commissioning to take part in some war games off the west coast. I have become a golf and fishing buddy of the admiral in charge of the west Pacific. He's invited us into the Command Center to watch the games."

Now Tom really did perk up. "That sounds like a vacation worthy of the drive west," he said. "When and where?"

"The commissioning will be at 12 noon on June 17th at the San Diego Navy Base. I'll meet you about 10 o'clock in the lobby of the COMPACWEST headquarters building. The gate guard can direct you. Just show him your ID. But don't be late; the Navy may be old fashioned, but even they tend to start ceremonies on time."

"I'll be there," Tom said, and hung up the phone. Now Tom had something to look forward to. His day had brightened considerably.

Promptly at 9:30 on the 17th, Tom pulled up at the gate of the San Diego Navy Base. He showed the guard his FBI ID. After a short wait while his identity was confirmed, he received his base pass and directions to the command building.

Tom parked his Mustang at the side of the building and made his way around to the lobby. Once inside, there was no sign of Fred. Tom was immediately challenged by a guard. He again showed his FBI ID and the guard took a few minutes to consult his approved guest list. The guard apologized his the delay and gave Tom his ID and an all-access pass to the building.

In a few minutes Fred appeared and took charge of things. He picked up his own pass, then he ushered Tom out of the building and across the street toward the docks. About two blocks down was a two-story white building. Tom never found out what was in the building, because Fred led Tom to the rear of the building. There hung a fire escape ladder that reached to the roof. Fred pulled the ladder down and urged Tom to climb up. Fred followed Tom to the roof.

Fed gestured toward the front of the building where he had placed a pair of lawn chairs and a small table. As soon as the two were seated, Fred produced a six-pack of ice-cold beer from a cooler.

"How's this for viewing in comfort?" Fred asked, as he handed Tom a can of beer. "Oh, that crazy looking thing down there at the dock in front of us is the new frigate."

Tom looked, but didn't quite believe his eyes. The 'ship' was barely 60 yards long and 20 yards wide. It was somewhat boxy and it sat low in the water. There was a long tube on each side of the vessel next to the superstructure. A large caliber gun was located just in front of the superstructure and what looked to be two gatling guns were mounted on either side of the bow. The rear area appeared to be relatively uncluttered. The prow appeared fairly normal. But the top was angled inward, not outward as had been customary. The superstructure was much more angular than usual.

"Those *are* gatling guns," Fred affirmed. "They fire about 130 rounds a minute. That's a six- inch deck gun. The tubes are for Comanche missiles. Besides those, there are two torpedo tubes below water. This little ship has been designed to get in and get out quickly and do as much damages as possible in between.

"Oh, yes," he added, "This baby is also a hydrofoil with ram jet assisted propulsion. It can cruise at 35 knots and its max speed is above 45. But the Navy won't admit how much above. It can also stifle its engine noise to barely audible at low speed."

"Phew!" was Tom's only comment.

At that moment a black car turned onto the pier and stopped beside the frigate. The driver got out and opened the back door. A lone man in a dark suit got out, walked to the frigate and boarded it. He quickly disappeared from sight.

"Phew!" Now it was Fred's turn. "That looked like the HS Secretary, Alan Burke. Rumor has it he was the driving force behind the speedy development of the frigate."

The car pulled off toward the end of the dock and parked. Soon more cars came and unloaded their

VIP's and parked at the end of the dock. The last two cars were flying flags with stars. Fred identified the Chief of Naval Operations and the COMPACWEST Admiral Lewis.

Secretary Burke exited the frigate and joined the others at the dock. The commissioning ceremony was about to start. The frigate's crew followed by the Captain emerged from inside the ship. They were all decked out in dress whites. The crew, about twenty of them, stood at attention along the side. The Captain passed down the gangplank to the dock. He saluted the assembled admirals and remained at attention.

At that point Tom and Fred sat back and enjoyed their beer as the sound from below wafted weakly up to them. While the ceremony was continuing, a submarine from an adjacent dock set sail and passed out of the harbor just beyond the frigate. Tom grabbed his binoculars. He was far more interested in the sub than the frigate. 'All those ballistic missiles,' he thought.

When the ceremony concluded, Tom was still watching through his binoculars. The crew headed back below decks. The Captain, who was actually a commander, and the admirals exchanged salutes. The crowd dispersed as their cars returned to pick them up. The captain remained. He was shaking hands with Secretary Burke. The latter gave the captain a brief hug about the shoulders and waved to him as he returned to his ship. 'Strange,' Tom thought.

The Frigate's engines came to life. They really *were* quiet. Crew members in work uniforms appeared on deck to cast off lines. The order to cast off came from the bridge over hidden speakers. The Frigate, free of her restraints, made an immediate U-turn and headed toward the end of the dock.

Chapter 7

Intelligence

Fred was ready to get back to the command center, but Tom hesitated, watching the Frigate on its way out to the channel. Then he called to Fred, "Hey, Fred, what's up, now?"

Fred turned and looked at the Frigate. Instead of turning left at the end of the dock and heading for the open sea, the Frigate turned right, back into the bay.

"Captain must have forgotten how to get out of the harbor," Fred mused. He and Tom continued watching as the Frigate turned into the next dock and proceeded to tie up opposite a large building.

A seaman left the Frigate holding a file folder and went into the building. Now both Fred and Tom were watching through their binoculars. Men started coming out of the building with carts loaded with torpedoes and several crates of what looked to be ammunition and a couple of longer crates. The crew of the Frigate emerged from the ship and assisted in the loading process. Eventually, the torpedoes and the ammunition crates disappeared into the Frigate.

"Ammunition load," Fred said. "That must be the arsenal. Guess they couldn't load ammunition until the ship was commissioned."

"There seems to be some sort of a disagreement," Tom observed.

Two seamen were arguing about something. The one from the boat was waving a sheet of paper; the other was pointing at the long crates. The seaman with the paper shouted back at the ship. They were too far away. Tom couldn't hear what he was saying. The Frigate Captain appeared, came down the gangplank and entered into the discussion.

The Frigate Chief and what appeared to be a Chief from the Arsenal each presented their opinions. The Captain looked at the paper and looked at the crates. Then he listened to the Arsenal Chief. The Arsenal Chief won.

The crew from the Frigate proceeded to open the crates and load two large cylinders onto the Frigate and insert them into the tubes on the sides of the ship.

Fred and Tom folded up the chairs and table. Then they tied them and the cooler into a bundle and lowered the bundle to the ground. They scampered down the fire escape and headed back to the Headquarters building. Fred stashed the bundle in his car and he and Tom went inside the building.

They showed their passes to the guard and were directed down to the Command Center in the basement. Their passes were checked again at the door of the Command Center, then they were passed inside.

The Command Center was a long room with a large table in the middle surrounded by many chairs.

On the wall at the far end of the table was a giant screen. At the moment the screen displayed the Pacific Ocean off the California coast. There were three red symbols visible on the screen. Two up by San Francisco heading west. One closer to Los Angeles heading northwest. A green symbol was still in the middle of San Diego. Presumably, it was the Frigate.

Admiral Lewis was seated at the head of the table facing the wall, with an interactive version of the large display imbedded into the table in front of him. Other individuals were scattered around the table.

"Well, now that you two are here," Admiral Lewis said with a chuckle, "I suppose I can start the briefing."

Tom and Fred hastily took seats at the table.

"This war games exercise," the Admiral began, "is two fold. First, it will test our ability to deter an enemy ship from penetrating our coastal defenses, and, second, it will test the ability of our new Frigate to do just that. The participants in the exercise are: an aircraft carrier, to provide aerial observation and deterrence, a destroyer, which should be the basic equivalent of the Frigate in a larger package, for surface interdiction, and a submarine, for underwater detection and interdiction."

As each ship was mentioned by the Admiral, its symbol on the display blinked.

"The exercise will actually begin at noon tomorrow, Zulu time, about 16 hours from now. In the meantime, the ships will get into position. The exercise will take place in an area approximately 500 miles square between San Francisco and Los Angeles. The Frigate will assume a position somewhere outside that boundary and at the appointed time begin to penetrate the area. Its mission is to get sufficiently close to the west coast to launch a Comanche into a specified area of the Mohave Desert near China Lake. The China Lake facility will monitor the strike, if it happens, and determine the accuracy of the hit. Only dummy warheads will be used in the exercise, of course.

"The other ships will attempt to interdict the Frigate and/or prevent the launch of the Comanche. The Frigate will capitulate whenever a shooting solution is tendered.

"Once the Frigate leaves the San Diego harbor, it will switch its IFF code to a special frequency, which only we will be able to monitor. That way we will be able to monitor the location of all the ships, and planes, at all times and determine the success or failure of any special tactics being used.

"You all are free to stick around, but the real action will not begin until about 0200 tomorrow."

While the Admiral had been talking, Tom was only listening with half an ear. He was watching the Frigate as it left the San Diego harbor and entered the Pacific.

According to maritime law, any ship entering or exiting the harbor had to stay within a narrow channel some three miles long. This was done so that larger arriving and departing ships would not interfere with smaller local vessels, and vice-versa. Tom was watching the Frigate as it approached the end of this channel.

All logic said that the Frigate would turn on its special IFF frequency and veer to the northwest to position itself for the start of the exercise. But, when the Frigate reached the end of the channel, Tom was certain that he saw the Frigate turn toward the south, just before its signal disappeared completely from the display.

The Admiral had finished his explanation and was in conversation with another visitor. Fred was also engaged in a side conversation. Something about a golf game. Tom decided to interrupt.

"Uh, Admiral," he began tentatively, "What happened to the Frigate?"

Admiral Lewis, somewhat irritated, glanced back at the display. The Frigate wasn't there. "Must be some mistake," he mumbled and reached for a phone. After a short conversation, he was more concerned. "It looks as though the Frigate is no longer broadcasting on its assigned IFF frequency," he announced. "Nor did it switch to its special exercise frequency, either."

"Uh, Admiral," Tom began again, "Can we review the display as the Frigate approached the end of the channel? Maybe in smaller scale."

The Admiral was not happy that Tom was butting in, but gave the order. In a minute or so, the display went blank. Then it switched to a small scale rendering of the Frigate in the channel. It showed the Frigate's signal as it came to the end of the channel. Tom watched carefully; he wanted to see if his first inclination was correct.

The blip indicating the Frigate was nearing the end of the channel when it veered slightly to the left and disappeared.

"Play that again," Tom suggested, "And watch the Frigate's signal carefully."

They did play it again. And, again, the Frigate's signal veered slightly to the left just before it disappeared. This time, everyone noted it.

Comments erupted around the table. "Did it sink?" "Was it damaged by something?" What about a collision?" "Is that Captain playing games with us?" The truth was, nobody knew. Finally, a good suggestion: "Can we get Air/Sea Rescue out there to look around?"

The Admiral acknowledged that as a good idea and put in a call. "They will have a helicopter airborne in ten minutes", he announced.

Tom nudged Fred. "I wan to check something," he whispered. "I'll be right back."

To rose and quietly left the Command Center.

Chapter 8

Comanches

Tom didn't bother with his car. He jogged as quickly as he could down to the pier where the arsenal was located. He wanted to get there before the day crew went home for the day.

When he got to the arsenal building and poked his nose in the door he caused something of a clamor. "Who are you and what are you doing around here?" Tom was challenged by a seaman.

"I happen to be an FBI agent, with a pass from Admiral Lewis," Tom tried. "I'm sorry I startled you, but I didn't see a guard posted."

"I am the guard," the seaman announced. "May I see your identification?"

Tom displayed his ID and pass. The guard scanned it dutifully. "I'm sorry, sir," the guard apologized. "What can I do for you?"

"I'd like to speak with the Chief who dealt with the Frigate this afternoon, if he's still here."

"He's still here," the guard assured Tom.

The guard escorted Tom to the Chief's office and introduced him.

"What is it you want to know?" the Chief asked warily.

"I saw you discussing something with the crew of the Frigate that finally involved the Captain. I was wondering just what the problem was."

The Chief was astonished at that revelation. But decided that discretion was called for at the moment.

"It was just a little misunderstanding about part of their order," the Chief said.

"That much was obvious, Chief," Tom admonished him. "What was it about?".

"We filled their order as it was written, but they had a disagreement with the fill."

"You are being deliberately evasive, Chief," Tom insisted. "If this matter is classified higher than Top Secret, just tell me so and I will get Admiral Lewis over here to discuss it with you. Otherwise, I expect a straight answer, and I expect it now."

"Well, sir," the Chief was obviously impressed, "the fact of the matter is that I was confused, too. Something is going on and I can't quite figure it out.'"

"I gathered that much," Tom said. "Just what was the disagreement? And don't worry, I am not here to hang anyone. I just need the facts."

"Well, the fact is," the Chief said. "Over a week ago we were alerted and ordered special supplies for this particular mission – the war games, I mean. They just had to have these Comanches with dummy warheads – just enough explosive to make a bang and scatter some dust. Heck, the missile itself would do more damage on impact than the charge would."

"The Admiral has already briefed us on the Comanches," Tom said.

"Aye, sir," the Chief continued. "Well, we were ready to roll them out to the ship when they docked. Then this Chief comes off the ship with this order. I can show you a copy of it, if you would like, sir. I always keep a copy of every order we fill."

"Thank you, Chief," Tom interrupted him, "But what about the Comanches?"

"Aye, sir," the Chief said apologetically. "Well, the order the chief showed a whole lot more than we were expecting. Instead of dummy Comanches, type Q is what we had in stock for them, the orders specifically called for type E. And they also called for ammunition for the gattlings and the deck gun."

"Why was that a problem?" Tom asked.

"Well, for two reasons," the Chief explained. "First, that wasn't what we expected. But that really isn't important – we can usually go with the flow, as it were, and we had most everything in stock. Second, and more important, we didn't have any type E Comanches in stock."

"But I saw you roll out two Comanche crates before the argument started," Tom pointed out. "If you didn't have any type E, what were you offering them?"

"Well, sir," the Chief patiently explained, "the type E had recently been recalled and replaced by the type J. We had turned in all our type E's and had already received the new type J missiles. I had the guys roll out two of the type J's."

"And that caused the argument?" Tom asked.

"Aye, sir," the Chief intoned. "The Chief from the Frigate demanded that we fill the order exactly and wouldn't listen to any explanation. I told him we couldn't fill that part of the order, and he called for the Captain.

"Captain was a pretty nice guy. He listened and looked at the order and at the crates. Finally, he accepted my explanation and his crew loaded the missiles. Frankly, I'm glad that Frigate isn't going to stationed here after the exercise. That Chief is a heck of a guy to dicker with; your pardon, sir, but that's the truth."

"Thank you, Chief," Tom said. "That wasn't so hard, was it? Oh, by the way, just what is the difference between the 'E' and 'J' types?"

"To be honest, sir," the Chief apologized, "I don't really know. I asked the same question when the recall was issued. The only answer I ever got was that they had made an improvement in the navigation and guidance system. Just what that change was, that was real hush-hush. No one knew, or wanted to talk about it."

"Thanks again, Chief," Tom said. "Oh, just for my curiosity, what kind of weapon is the J-type?"

"Tactical thermo-nuclear." The Chief answered softly. Then he added, "Big boom!"

"In that case," Tom asked, "just how are the crates marked?"

"They have the name and official designation of the missile," the Chief ticked off the data, "the type codes and the production data. Pretty standard stuff."

Tom probed further. "Any indication that it is a thermo-nuclear device?"

"Oh, no, Sir," the Chief insisted. That is considered classified information.

Tom thanked the Chief for his help, turned and made a bee-line for the Command Building and the briefing room.

Chapter 9

The Frigate

Commander Burke was just changing into his dress whites when a crew member knocked on his door and informed him that there was a civilian wearing a suit onboard who wanted to talk to him.

The Commander quickly finished dressing, then he went forward and climbed the ladder to the Combat Information Center below the bridge. From there he could exit to the deck. Standing there, visually inspecting the Frigate was a familiar figure.

"Good morning, Dad," Commander Burke said.

The man turned. "Good morning, Son," he said. "You look very spiffy. And already a Commander and Captain of your own ship. Things must be going very well for you."

"Can't complain, Dad," Commander Richard Burke replied. "I'm glad you're going to be on hand for the commissioning!"

"Well, I would have come for that regardless," Secretary Burke said, "but that isn't the only reason I am here. Is there somewhere we can speak privately?"

Commander Burke was perplexed and curious. "Come on down to my cabin," he suggested. Then he led his father down below decks. Once they were in the Captain's cabin, Commander Burke closed the door and turned to face his father.

"Sorry the conditions are so cramped," he said, "but we lack some of the amenities of your standard destroyer."

"I'm fine," Secretary Burke said. Then he continued in hushed tones, "Son, there has been a change in your orders. The war game has been changed from a penetration exercise to a fox-and-hounds exercise. These are your new orders." He took a sheaf of papers from his inside pocket and handed them to his son.

"You are to completely disregard your previous orders," the Secretary said, "and follow these explicitly. Your Frigate will play the fox. Immediately after the commissioning, you will proceed to the arsenal on pier three. There, you will present the munitions annex from your new orders. See that it is filled exactly as written – no substitutions or alterations. You will then proceed, as rapidly as possible to the set of coordinates listed in your orders. You may use any route you deem advisable, but you must ensure that you avoid all of the 'hounds' sent to pursue you and trap you. En route you will load the 'target' coordinates contained in your orders into the Comanches. When you reach your destination, or at any time you are captured or disabled, launch the Comanches. At that point, if possible, you will return to San Diego by any route you choose. You may also surrender to any opposing force after you have launched your missiles.

"I suggest you read over your orders now in case you have any questions. Some of the terms may appear rather drastic, but I assure you that they are absolutely essential for the correct completion of the exercise."

Captain Burke scanned the orders. They seemed to be properly prepared. They had all the right signatures and citations. Then he actually read them. As he paged through the orders, his visage changed from happy and confident to worried and tentative. Finally, he folded them and set them on his desk.

"From what I gather," the Captain said, "our sole objective is to get to point alpha and launch our Comanches. We are supposed to do so by avoiding all contact with other naval vessels or aircraft, foreign or domestic. To do this we are to run deaf, dumb and blind; no radio, no IFF, no lights. Did I miss anything?"

"Yes, you did, Secretary Burke replied. "If any vessel or aircraft is in a position to prevent you from achieving your goal, you are to eliminate the threat. There is no retreat and no surrender until the missiles are launched."

"This doesn't sound like much of a game," the Commander said. "Are you sure this is just an exercise? I didn't see that last caveat in the order."

"It's there implicitly," the Secretary said. Then he quietly added, "I know I am asking a lot of you, son. Please believe me, this is no joke. The proper completion of this exercise is a matter of national importance. I assume, as a Naval officer, you are prepared to follow orders that may place you life in danger. I sincerely regret having to place you in such a position."

At that moment, a crew member knocked on the door and announced, "Captain, they are ready to start the ceremony. The crew is standing by."

"I must take my leave now," the Secretary said. He reached out a hand to shake his son's, then drew him close in a tight embrace. The Secretary released his son, turned and made his way topside and off the ship.

The Captain grabbed his hat, checked the crew and followed them topside and then he went down the gangplank to the group already formed on the dock. Standing at attention in the warm California sun made the commissioning ceremony seem to last forever. But all things come to an end, even Naval ceremonies. In due time Captain Burke was again boarding his ship.

"Chief," he yelled, "we're now in the working Navy. Be ready to cast off in twenty minutes."

In exactly twenty minutes, the Captain, now wearing standard fatigues with a brand new "Captain" ball cap, gave the order to cast off all lines. Using the Frigate's thrusters, he maneuvered the little ship in a 180° turn and headed over to the base arsenal on pier 3.

When they had tied up at the arsenal, the Captain handed the Chief the Weapons annex from his new operations plan and told him to get the ammo load post haste. Captain Burke was still going over the first phase of the operations order when the Chief called him out to the dock.

"What's up, Chief?" he asked as he joined a small group clustered around a couple of Comanche crates.

"Sir," the Frigate Chief said, "they don't have what our orders call for and are trying to foist off some substitute."

"Captain," the Arsenal Chief explained, these aren't just 'some substitute'. They are a replacement for the type E your orders call for. We had to turn in all our E's and got these to replace them. If you want Comanches, this is all we've got."

Captain Burke examined the sticker on the crate. It appeared that they would do, if that was all the arsenal had. He told the Chief to load them and went back on board.

As soon as the ammunition had been stored, Captain Burke spoke to the crew. "This is the Captain," he announced. "Now hear this. We thought we were going out on a simple penetration mission. A 'war game' with no real danger involved whether we succeeded or failed. That has changed. As you noticed, we have just loaded live ammunition. Our first mission is no longer a simple war game. Our new orders require us to sail to a specific location and launch our Comanches. From what I know of our mission, just about everybody out there is going to try to stop us. Presumably, they are also going to be using live ammunition. This mission could legitimately be fatal to all of us. I am going to wait five minutes, before I order all lines to be cast off. If any crew member wants to leave the ship now, I will not deem him to be a coward or a deserter. That is all."

Exactly five minutes later, the Captain ordered all lines cast off and turned the Frigate toward the harbor entrance and the wide Pacific Ocean. While they were getting underway, the Chief came up to him and whispered, "All the crew remained on board, Sir."

As they approached the end of the channel, the Captain, announced to the crew, "This is the Captain. Team A: General Quarters. Team B: Stand down. All crew, prepare for silent running."

Then he made a series of announcements to the crew: "Comm, cease all voice communication, do not respond to any incoming messages! I want no outgoing communications. Radar and sonar, man your scopes at all times. I want to know what is going on out there. Engine Room, prepare to go hydro. From now on, we are on a war footing."

The Frigate continued slowly moving out of the channel. If anyone was watching, they would detect no sense of urgency or nervousness. Just before they reached the end of the channel, the Captain ordered: "Engine Room, initiate hydro drive, extend our legs, full speed ahead. Comm, turn off the IFF now. Nav, begin the course I laid out for us."

The Frigate suddenly transformed into a hydrofoil and rose magnificently on two extended legs, bit into the water and greatly increased its speed. It also made a sharp turn to the left and began following the coastline south.

Chapter 10

A Warning

Tom raced through the entrance of the Headquarters Building and down to the Command Center. The guard on the door wisely opened it when he saw Tom running down the hall. Tom came to a screeching halt at the entrance to the room. He walked in normally, but his heart was still racing.

Tom resumed his seat at the table, looked around to get the current lay of the land. The display still showed the three interdiction ships and an additional blue blip moving around near the entrance to the channel. He then turned to Fred.

"Any change?" he asked quietly.

"None," Fred replied.

"What's the blue blip all about?" Tom asked.

"That's the Air/Sea Rescue chopper," Fred whispered. "He can't find any trace of the Frigate."

Tom looked over at Admiral Lewis. He was in an agitated conversation with the captain seated next to him. Tom tried to wait for a break in the conversation, but none presented itself. Tom's sense of urgency finally got the better of him.

"Excuse me, Admiral," Tom interrupted the Admiral's conversation.

"Huh?" the Admiral looked around for the source of the interruption.

"Excuse me," Tom repeated. "But I believe I have some new information, which may be critical to our discussion."

"What 'new information'?" the Admiral asked.

"I believe you said in your initial briefing," Tom summarized, " that the Frigate was to launch two dummy Comanches into the Mohave Desert. Am I correct?"

"Yes, that is what the exercise orders called for," Admiral Lewis conceded. He was still unhappy that his conversation had been interrupted, even if it hadn't been getting anywhere.

"Are you aware," Tom asked, "that the Frigate just picked up two Type J Comanche missiles from your arsenal?"

"What is the significance of that?" the Admiral almost shouted. "Young man, neither I, nor anyone else at this table is an expert on Comanches. Please speak clearly!"

"I beg your pardon, Admiral," Tom apologized. "The Frigate picked up two tactical nuclear weapons, along with a full load of torpedoes and ammunition for the deck guns. I don't think they are exactly following your exercise plans."

"What?" the Admiral bellowed. "You're out of your mind. Where did you get that cockeyed idea?"

"From the Chief of your arsenal," Tom explained calmly. "I just came from there. In case you are interested, here is a copy of the munitions order the Frigate presented." Tom placed a single sheet of paper on the table in front of the Admiral.

The Admiral picked up the paper, scrutinized it carefully and, finally, deemed it authentic. He sat back in his chair and everyone at the table, who were all focused on the single sheet of paper, ceased their conversations and anxiously awaited the Admiral's explanation.

"This casts an entirely new light on the matter," the Admiral said quietly. "While it does answer a few questions, it raises a whole boatload of new ones.

"I think we can reliably assume that the Frigate is no longer pursuing the exercise we laid out for this war game. The crew obviously have a new set of orders. I can assure you that they didn't come from me. But finding the Frigate – and stopping it – now takes on a much greater urgency. I am open for suggestions."

Tom had been thinking about the situation. He couldn't help but feel that his recent assignment and this event were somehow related.

"Admiral," Tom said, "I think we are all pretty familiar with torpedoes, and deck guns, but could you fill us in on the general specifics for the Comanche missile?"

"Of course," the Admiral answered. He looked down the table for some technical help. "Commander Andrews, can you answer the question about the missiles?" he asked.

"Yes, Admiral," the Commander responded, "It is a relatively short range tactical nuclear weapon with a single payload. It is controlled through the GPS system. It can be launched from the tubes that you saw on either side of the Frigate."

"How short a range?" Fred asked.

"About 400 nautical miles," the Commander answered. "It can travel in a high arc for less distance or in low level straight flight for greater distance. It also depends on whether you want an air burst or a ground burst. It has a limited cruise capability."

Fred looked over at Tom who was sitting quietly, his brow furrowed, deep in thought. "You've got something brewing, haven't you?" he whispered.

"I have a few thoughts," Tom admitted. "That is, if none of the experts have anything to offer."

"You seem to have been the only one on top of this so far," Admiral Lewis conceded. "Give us the benefit of your thoughts. We can always give them back to you, if we don't like them."

"Well," Tom began, "if we assume that the Frigate captain has orders to launch his Comanches at a specific target from a specific point, we have to assume that his primary goal is to protect his ship until he has completed his mission. That is probably what the torpedoes and deck gun ammo are for. For the moment, let's assume that he did turn left at the end of the channel. That little slip may be our biggest clue as to what happens next ... "

"Wait a minute," the Admiral interrupted, "Why should we assume that?"

"Because," Tom replied, "The Frigate captain knew he had an aircraft carrier out of Honolulu to his west, a submarine due north, and a destroyer floating around between them. He is not likely to turn into certain danger, when he can go south, where all he has to deal with is the Mexican navy.

"So, assuming he turns south, we have only one choice open to us at this time. Send that sub after him as fast as it can travel. With orders to destroy the Frigate upon contact."

Everyone at the table just stared at Tom. How could he suggest destroying the Frigate, the Navy's newest and most modern ship? Not to mention the probable loss of the entire crew.

Tom sensed the problem. No one had to say it out loud.

"The Frigate captain may be able to launch from more than one point, if it is necessary to ensure completion of his mission. He probably knows this is a suicide mission, anyway. If he detects an 'enemy' he cannot destroy or out run, I would bet that he will launch if there is any chance at all to succeed."

"I will order the sub to give chase immediately," Admiral Lewis said. "Perhaps I can get some aircraft in close enough to get a fix on the Frigate without scaring the Captain."

Fred now entered the fray, "We really need to figure out what his target, or targets, might be. What looks good within 400 NM of his probable course?"

Admiral Lewis had given the order to contact the sub. He now switched the display to the Pacific coast south of San Diego. Baja California dominated the screen.

"Admiral," Tom suggested, "can you plot a box 400 NM wide on either side of the Baja west coast?"

The boxes appeared on the screen. They were not immediately helpful. They covered an area from San Francisco to Durango, Mexico and from the western coast of the US and Baja California to southern Nevada and Western Arizona.

"How much damage can the Comanches do?" Fred asked.

The Captain answered, "They are meant to take out a ship or small, well-fortified position. Maybe a village or a small neighborhood in a big city. About one or two square miles of total destruction, depending on the materials being used on the ground. They are virtually radiation free; no contamination."

'One square mile', 'village', 'western Arizona' These comments bounced around in Tom's head for a few minutes. Then he put them together!

"Admiral," Tom exclaimed, "I think I know what the target is!"

"What?" the question came from several around the table.

"I can't tell you, right now" Tom replied. "And I could be completely wrong. But, if I am right, I need to get back to Arizona immediately. Admiral can you get me a jet ride back to Tucson? Right now?!"

"You can use my plane," Admiral Lewis answered. "It's over at the Sea/Air strip. I'll call them and it will be ready by the time you get there. Will you be able to determine what the target actually is and report back to us?"

"No, Admiral," Tom confessed. "This is simply a mercy flight. If I am right about the target, I want to save as many of the people involved as I can. It is still imperative that you stop the Frigate by any means you can. Search on both sides of Baja California."

With that cryptic comment, Tom rushed out of the Headquarters Building to his car and broke a few speed limits on his way around the base to the Air/Sea field.

Chapter 11

The Frigate

Following the flurry of activity as the Frigate left the channel, the little ship rose up and rushed south at full speed. Captain Burke wanted to put as much distance as possible between himself and any likely pursuers. By now he was sure that the Admiral would be hosting a tense meeting in the Command Center. The Captain had set a radar and sonar watch. Neither had reported any significant contacts.

Captain Burke went over his orders for the fifth or sixth time. He had a certain destination to reach and a specific action he was to take when he reached that destination. How he got there was left to his own ingenuity. He studied the charts of the Baja Peninsula. There were virtually no significant towns on the west coast. His problem was whether or not to maintain maximum speed until he reached *Cabo San Lucas* or to lay over and rest the crew, knowing the delay would give his pursuers a chance to catch up.

The last fix he had on the exercise sub placed it some 300 miles from San Diego. Even at full speed it wasn't as fast as the Frigate. The carrier was not a potent threat. Its jets were much faster than the Frigate, but it was much further away. And the jets had a limited range

But what about the bases in Southern California? Among them, they had a full compliment of aircraft. Yes, that was the greater danger. Captain Burke knew he could not run away from them. Those planes he would have to outsmart.

He made up his mind. He went back to the bridge and checked the Frigate's course and speed. They were hugging the Baja coast. In eight hours or so they would close on a large cove almost in the middle of the peninsula guarded by an outcropping of land.

"Alright, Evans," Captain Burke said, "I'll take the con. You take a break and ask Lt. Baker to join me on the Bridge."

Lt Jeff Baker quickly joined the Captain. "What's the plan, Captain?"

"We're going to hold up in one of the coves up ahead so everyone can rest," the Captain explained. "Then, about mid-morning tomorrow, if all is clear, we'll break out and continue south at high speed. I plan to reach the Navy base at *Cabo* just after dark and blow right through. Then we continue straight up the Gulf. If we can make it to the islands by Hernando, we can launch without a problem."

"Then what," Jeff asked quietly. "By that time they will have us penned in for sure."

"I intend to set you and the crew off on the mainland south of Hernando," the Captain said. "Then I'm going to take the Frigate into battle, for as long as the two of us last. I'm going to try to force them to sink her. That way they will think she went down with all hands. That should give you sufficient time to make a clean break."

Jeff looked like he was about to object, but the Captain interrupted his thoughts. "Look, Jeff," he said, "I want to handle as much of this as I can. You and the crew will be able to claim that you were not involved – literally and truthfully. Just keep the crew calm and on their toes."

Jeff nodded solemnly. He stood by and provided moral support, and several cups of black coffee.

Several hours later, Captain Burke announced, "Here's the cove. Let's see if we can find a nice small inlet to hide in."

The Captain shifted the Frigate out of hydroplane mode and slowed it to a creep. He steered toward a collection of small inlets. After a brief search he found one he liked, just wide enough for the Frigate to maneuver in and deep enough to hide the entire ship. He very carefully backed the Frigate into the inlet and dropped anchor.

"Okay, Jeff," the Captain said, "Tell the crew to break out the camouflage and cover her up. Then we can settle down for a good meal and get some sleep. Set a four hour watch, just in case, and roust me out in eight hours, if I'm not up."

The rest of the night was ominously calm. Captain Burke slept fitfully and was up just as dawn broke. He took a quick shower, donned a clean uniform and went to the galley for a cup of coffee. Then he went to the CIC for an status update.

Radar had been quiet all night. Because they were in a small cove, the sonar was not able to provide any information. Captain Burke had the chilling thought that the sub could be lurking just outside the cove, waiting for the Frigate to emerge. 'No,' his rational mind insisted, 'the sub couldn't have reached us, yet.'

In good time the crew rose and ate breakfast with large volumes of strong black coffee. The cooks prepared sandwiches for a meal on the run. By mid-morning it was time to make that run.

The captain gave the orders from the bridge. "B-Team, general quarters. A-Team retrieve and stow the camouflage then stand down." The light-weight camouflage fabric was peeled off the prow and rear of the ship and stowed in a special aft compartment. Then it was time to get moving.

"Rig for silent running," the Captain announced. "All ahead slow. Sharp eyes on the radar and sonar!"

The Frigate moved slowly out of the cove where it had been hiding and into the Pacific. Then, beyond the outcropping, it turned south. The Captain waited for long range radar and sonar reports. When all reports were negative, it was time to lower the hydrofoil and resume full speed ahead.

Several hours later, as darkness descended over the water, the lights of *El Cabo* were visible in the distance. Something else was also visible.

"CIC to Captain," the radio sounded, "Sonar contact southwest, maximum range. It looks like a sub." Captain Burke turned the bridge over to Lt Baker and went down to the CIC. When he got there, both Radar and sonar were busy. He looked at the sonar reading. The sub was just barely in range, but it appeared to be positioned to intercept the Frigate at *Cabo*. They were not an immediate threat, but they could be in firing range by the time the two met at *Cabo*. He would have to outwit them, if he could. All of a sudden, this mission was becoming all too real.

The radar screen was more urgent. Aircraft were flying a search pattern west of the Frigate. Captain Burke smiled. Apparently the US had not negotiated an intrusion in to Mexican waters. The aircraft, and any surface vessels, would be forced to stay at least twelve miles off the coast. With the Frigates anti-radar design and low profile, they might not be able to see her from that distance. Even if they could see the Frigate, they were making no effort to interdict it.

Captain Burke had another chilling thought. 'What if the sub and the aircraft were talking to each other?' To his knowledge, that tactic had never been tried. Now would not be a good time – for the Frigate – if they were.

There was something else on the radar – smaller ships far ahead. He turned to the Chief in charge of the CIC. "Chief, pipe the radar and sonar output to the Bridge. Then, keep a sharp eye on our sensors. Advise me immediately in there is any change in the direction or attitude of the sub or planes."

Back on the bridge, the Captain called for the crew to prepare for silent running. The engines were immediately throttled back and the hydrofoil raised up into the body of the ship. Guiding the ship by the seat of his pants, in the dark, was not the easiest thing to do, but it was all he dared do at the moment. He moved the Frigate as close to the coast as was reasonably possible and mentally crossed his fingers. As the Frigate neared the harbor, at *Cabo San Lucas*, the Captain slowed even more and prepared to thread his way among the moored yachts and fishing vessels.

He briefed his Exec on the latest developments. "Sub approaching rapidly from the southwest and aircraft circling directly to the west," the Captain explained. "I am going to try to sneak through the harbor to confuse them as to who is who. Then, maybe, we can outrun them up into the Gulf."

The radar display showed a blip moving toward the Frigate from inside the harbor. The strong, throaty sound of its diesel engine wafting over the water soon confirmed that it was likely a Mexican patrol boat. Captain Burke activated the deck guns and linked the six-inch gun to the radar blip. The gun began to automatically track the on-coming vessel.

The Frigate was able to enter the harbor unmolested and Captain Burke heaved one great sigh of relief. It appeared that were going to make it. Then the patrol boat suddenly picked up speed and turned directly toward the Frigate. "The sub or the planes must be feeding data to the Mexicans," Burke grumbled.

Captain Burke's finger rested easily on the gun trigger. The sub and the planes were boxing in the Frigate. Burke couldn't swing out to sea and he couldn't get by behind the patrol boat. The patrol boat would be upon him if he took the time to lower the hydroplane. Besides it was too crowded in the harbor to do that safely.

The consequences of his orders were rapidly becoming apparent. This really wasn't a 'war game' any more. It had turned deadly serious and Burke was in it up to his ears. It was too late to back off or change his mind, despite how much he suddenly wanted to. He used the hydro jets to greatly increase the Frigate's speed and the thrusters to swing the little ship around behind the approaching patrol boat. Then he pressed the gun trigger; two hundred yards away, the patrol boat disintegrated into a shower of glowing embers.

Burke slowed his speed and assumed the course the patrol boat had been following, south out of the harbor.

That did it. If there had been any doubt in his pursuers' minds before, it was no longer there. They knew exactly where the Frigate had been. Burke could only hope that his sudden maneuver would confuse them and they would believe that the patrol boat had sunk the Frigate. Not much of a chance, but it was better than nothing. The Frigate moved noisily through the harbor, trying to miss as many of the yachts and fishing vessels as possible. He actually did a pretty good job; only clipping a few boats in the process

As he neared the harbor exit, Captain Burke decided he might as well make it official. He turned out to sea, called for maximum speed and dropped the hydrofoils. The Frigate leaped forward and started skimming rapidly across the surface of the water.

A second patrol boat exited the harbor behind the Frigate, but it was soon lost in the Frigate's wake. East of the cape, there were some more yachts and fishing boats. These soon became fewer in number as the Frigate turned north into the Gulf of California.

The planes began dropping off the radar, but the sub doggedly remained at the edge of the Frigate's sonar range struggling to catch up.

Chapter 12

The Valley

For a small jet, Admiral Lewis' plane was the lap of luxury. Tom's only regret was that he had to leave his Mustang behind. Two hours after leaving California, the jet was descending for a landing at Davis Montham AFB in Tucson. Tom had called ahead from San Diego, one of his agents had brought a car to the airport. It was waiting on the tarmac at the transient hangar when Tom de-planed. As Tom had requested, it had been equipped with a blue light and siren.

"Good evening, Mr. Watson," Sandy greeted Tom, "Transportation, as requested."

"Hop in, Sandy," Tom responded. "I'll drop you back at the office, then I've got some driving to do." It was a quick drive up highway 200 to the Agency office, especially with the light and siren in action.

Tom dropped Sandy off at the office, retrieved a few papers from his files and took off again. He was only challenged once on his drive up to Winton. A State Trooper pulled in behind him, couldn't identify the plate and flipped on his blue light. When Tom saw the light behind him, he grabbed his radio microphone and switched to a common frequency.

"FBI Special Agent Tom Watson, Tucson Station Chief, I am traveling on official business and do not require assistance." Tom followed that with his badge number. It took a few seconds, but the trailing blue light blinked out as the trooper went off in search of more lucrative prey.

Tom managed to get all the way through Winton without exciting the attention of the local police. As he turned off on the reservation road, he pondered the best way to accomplish his intended mission. At the last minute, he turned right toward the casino, killed the blue light and proceeded on to Wakulla.

Tom stopped just outside of the town, turned on the car's spotlight and shined it down the street. He caught a glimpse of the sheriff's office and turned to the right to find a parking spot behind it. As Tom approached the office he saw the sheriff's old Jeep and pulled in beside it. He walked around the building and entered the front door of the sheriff's office.

The Sheriff was nowhere in sight, so Tom closed the door rather noisily. He could hear furniture moving in the back room. In a moment, Sheriff Billy Eagle emerged. He was still wearing his plaid shirt and jeans and riding boots, but the six-shooter was missing.

"Good evening, Sheriff," Tom began, "I didn't get to formally introduce myself the last time we met, so I thought it was about time. I am FBI Special Agent Tom Watson, Chief of the Tucson office."

Billy winced a bit when he heard Tom say 'FBI'. "I believe I told you who I was and what I do the last time we met. I probably should advise you that every time I have had dealings with the FBI it ended badly for the FBI. But, that said, what can I do for you?"

This was what Tom had come here for. He would much rather just go home and forget it. But, after his last visit to the Valley, he just couldn't do that. He put his determination in gear, and began.

"Sheriff, I have just come her from the San Diego Navy Base. It seems that the captain of the Navy's newest frigate has suddenly gone rogue. Apparently, he has been given secret orders without the Navy's knowledge. He has abandoned the scheduled war games exercise, loaded two thermo-nuclear missiles, and taken off for goodness knows where. I have reason to believe that his goal is to launch the missiles at the butte just west of here."

While Tom was talking, the Sheriff had been silently regarding the office floor. absentmindedly nodding a time or two. The moment Tom mentioned the butte, the Sheriff's head popped up and he stared at Tom with squinting eyes.

"Now just why would he want to do that?" the Sheriff asked. He was sure that he was facing some sort of kook.

"Because someone with proper authority told him to." Tom answered succinctly. Then he added, "The admiral in charge of the exercise, and to whom the Frigate is currently assigned, knew absolutely nothing about the change in orders."

"And just how do you know all about this?"

"The San Diego station chief and I had been invited to watch the commissioning of the new Frigate and the ensuing war games, Tom explained. "We were in the COMPACWEST commend center when the Frigate went rogue."

"I meant," the Sheriff said, "how do you know where the missiles are aimed?"

"I don't know for sure," Tom wavered. "But, considering the information I have, the butte is the logical target."

"What information?" Sheriff Billy was concerned – about the sanity of the individual standing in front of him.

"Look, Sheriff," Tom was getting irritated by the delay, "we are perfectly safe here, but those missiles are going to put a big hole in the ground inside that butte, turn the butte's walls into sand, and scare the hell out of anyone at what will be left of the casino. Your Shaman, and anyone inside the butte, is going to be just so many loose atoms. Take it from me, if you care a whit about those people out there, you would be better off finding a way to get them to safety.

"Yes," Tom answered the unasked question, "the Navy is doing its best to stop the Frigate, but it is facing the most modern ship in the inventory. And the people in the Command Center are as much in the dark as I am. My only advantage is that I think I know the Frigate's intended target."

"Assuming you're right," a somewhat subdued Billy asked, "how soon?"

" I can't say for sure," Tom replied. "I don't have the latest search data." The Sheriff winced. "But sometime in the next 24 hours, unless the Navy manages to stop them or delay them before they can launch."

"And your little visit out here a month ago was the start of all this," the Sheriff said. It was more of an accusation than a question.

"You know very well that is not true," Tom challenged, "The Director of the Bureau sent me out here to validate a set of coordinates. That wasn't his idea; someone asked him to do it. My guess is that 'someone' is the person who dreamed up this whole idea. If he could task the Director, he probably has the clout to get orders to the Frigate captain. I told you at the time that I was sending in a negative report. This is a copy of what I sent." Tom pulled the papers from the files out of his pocket and handed them to Billy.

Billy scanned the papers. His visage softened a bit as he read. "So where did this mysterious dude get these coordinates in the first place?" he asked.

"I don't know who he is, how he got the coordinates, or why he is doing this," Tom confessed. "I could even be completely wrong about the target. The Navy may be able to stop the Frigate. The missiles may misfire. But do you really want to take the chance? We have less than 24 hours to get the people in the butte to a place of safety. Don't you think it might be a good idea to get started?"

Sheriff Billy thought for a moment. This man had already been inside the Valley. He had seen and talked to the Elders. He even remembers them! None of that should ever have happened. It was in itself unusual. Obviously, the Elders had deemed it safe to let him remember and maybe they had seen something in him that they thought might be of value. If they were really in danger … ?

"Let's take my Jeep," The Sheriff suggested. He grabbed a .30 cal. Carbine off a wall mount as they went out the back door. "For coyotes", he said, waving the carbine..

The ride over to the butte was uneventful, if somewhat bumpy.

The Sheriff pulled into the opening of the canyon at the south end of the butte. "Wait here," he said to Tom. Then he walked into the canyon and over to the small cabin where he knocked on the door. Tom could see the door open and the Sheriff go inside. In a few minutes a figure emerged from the cabin. Tom could not make out who the person was in the dark. Too tall, he thought to be an Elder. The person slowly moved to the far end of the canyon, edged behind a large bush and disappeared.

Tom sat in the Jeep for many long minutes. Then he decided to get out and stretch his legs. He walked around the Jeep and admired the Sheriffs carbine. 'Coyotes!', he thought. He looked around and patted the pistol in his holster. 'The missiles', he thought. 'They could be on their way right now. Oh, well, I guess it's not the worst way to die.'

Tom caught some movement in the canyon out of the corner of his eye. He looked and saw the previous figure walking slowly toward the cabin. He still could not make out who the figure was, but it went up to the cabin and entered.

A few minutes later Billy Eagle left the cabin and walked back to the Jeep. He climbed in behind the wheel and just sat there. After a few very tense minutes he looked over at Tom and said, "They refuse to move out of the butte. They said that there are others ready to carry on if they should be killed. That it was better for the person who thought up this plot to believe they were all killed. They said it was not the worst way to die."

Tom did not reply.

Billy started the Jeep and drove back to Wakulla. When they were parked behind the Sheriff's office, Billy looked over at Tom and asked," Want to come in for a drink? I sure need one."

"No, thanks," Tom replied with a shake of his head. He got into his car and started to drive slowly back to Tucson. He kept his eye on the rear-view mirror all the way, looking for a red glow in the distance.

Chapter 13

Naomi to the Rescue

As soon as Red Hawk had left the Elder community, the Council got busy. They put their heads together to try to figure out a defense against the missiles. Someone suggested using the aliens' weapon to shoot it down. Another pointed out that by the time 'quick draw' actually focused on the missile it would be detonating over the Valley.

There were some other equally unsuitable suggestions. Mila finally said, "As we told Red Hawk, we have no adequate defense. And we aren't going to run from the Valley. Most of us would die in the process, anyway. All our food would be gone, so would all of our belongings and the content of the supply bunker. Some of the new Elders have been able to survive among the humans and the mutants appear to be quite at home with their human parents; but if all of the Elders from the Valley suddenly showed up, the results would not be good."

"Agreed, we have no defense," another Councilor offered, "but what about some kind of an offense? Is there some way we can prevent the missiles from being fired in the first place?"

"From what Red Hawk said," Mina replied, "the Navy is already trying to do just that. Without much success, so far. But maybe there is something we can do. We can at least find out which human thought up this and see to it that he never gets another chance. Maybe we'll get lucky."

Mina went into the back of the Council chambers and powered up the Kaleidoscope – the computer system used to communicate among the Elders. She placed an emergency call to Naomi and Serena in Washington, DC.

The shriek of the emergency Kaleidoscope call woke Naomi out of a sound sleep. She bolted out of bed and rushed out to the table where the computer sat. The shriek ended as soon as she acknowledged the message. Serena joined Naomi as she was scanning the message. Naomi waited until Serena had also digested the message.

When Serena had finished reading, she stared at Naomi with a very curious expression. "Are they saying they want us to save the Valley from some rogue Navy officer with a boat load of missiles?" she asked, not really believing the whole scenario.

"It seems to me," Naomi said, still a bit overwhelmed herself, "that we have two tasks: to find out who started this fiasco and to find some way to stop it from happening."

Serena was not reassured. "If the entire military force of the United States can't catch this guy, what chance do we have?"

"Maybe, if we put our minds to the task," Naomi replied, "we can ferret out some little tidbit that will give them a better chance. Mila said that the whole thing started when some FBI agent landed in the middle of the Valley trying to validate a set of coordinates. He said that his orders originated with the Director of the Bureau.

"But I don't think this was the FBI's idea in the first place. I'd bet that someone else in a higher position is responsible. I'd also bet that someone else had the power and ability to give orders to the Frigate captain. We need to find that someone and get to him – or her.

"We also need to get as much information about these missiles as we can. There may be some way to short-circuit them. And we have to do all of this in less than 12 hours."

"So," Serena suggested, "there is too much to do for both of us to take it all on. Why don't I go after the FBI Director. I can persuade him to tell me who gave him the original order. You go after your technical data on the missiles. Then we can meet and compare notes."

"That's going to complicate the transportation situation," Naomi pointed out. "You have to go downtown and I need to go to the Pentagon."

"Why don't I call Ali," Serena suggested. "I will feel more comfortable with him. And probably we won't have to go out of the District. You can call a town car. Those drivers will probably be more familiar with the Pentagon."

"Okay," Naomi agreed, "But I am sure glad we visited that ATM the other day. This little adventure is going to cost us. Let's get going!"

Serena arranged for the necessary transportation to meet them on the corner by the market. Naomi put their cell phones, money and a bit of fungus into a pair of cross-body bags. The weather was mild, so they decided to forgo clothes. They were a pain to remember and they always seemed to get in the way.

Ali was sleeping soundly when Serena called, but the promise of double his usual rate encouraged him to be at the market in fifteen minutes. The two Elders arrived at the pick-up corner next to the market about five minutes before Ali came roaring down the street. Serena left Naomi waiting and took off for the FBI headquarters building.

At that time of night, traffic was nonexistent and Ali made excellent time. The building was mostly dark when they pulled up in front. Serena told Ali to stick around and tried the front door. It was locked, but that didn't stop her. Serena was particularly adept at manipulating electronic devices. In a few minutes, she was into the building.

Serena stopped at the information desk in the lobby. She rummaged through the reference material until she came across a phone extension for the duty officer and dialed it. When someone answered the phone call, Serena made his day.

"I'm down in the lobby. I need the Director's home address. Now!" she said briskly.

In a matter of minutes, a uniformed security guard and two agents descended on the lobby where Serena was waiting. As soon as they came into view, Serena immobilized the security guard and the agent with the gun in his hand. Then she turned to the remaining agent.

"I told whomever answered the DO's extension that I need the Director's home address." Serena told the agent. "Get that for me and I'll give you back these two and leave quietly. Give me any grief and I'll make a statue out of you, too."

The agent hesitated, looked at Serena, as if assessing her potential threat, then he shrugged resignedly. "Let me make a call," he offered.

Serena shook her head. "I can't verify anything over the phone. Let's go to the personnel department where I can see his personal jacket. According to this directory, it's on the second floor. Lead on."

The agent reluctantly led the way to a bank of elevators. Once the two had entered an elevator, the agent reached over and pushed the door-shut button, the alarm button and the fourth floor button in rapid succession. The door shut, but there was no alarm and the elevator rose slowly to the second floor. As the door slid open, Serena said calmly, "Nice try. Suppose you stand guard here at the elevator. Step in the doorway."

The agent complied. Then he froze in place. "I'll be back in a few minutes," Serena told him. "Don't go away."

Serena prowled the hallway until she found the personnel office. A minute's manipulation of the lock and she was inside. There were dozens of filing cabinets. Serena wagered the folders were in alphabetical order. A glance at the certificates of excellence lining the wall led to the conclusion that the Director's name was Williams. A quick search led to the appropriate cabinet and drawer.

Serena opened the drawer and started thumbing through the folders. The fattest folder belonged to the Director and provided the information Serena was looking for. Serena made her way back to the lobby tidying up after herself. She walked the security guard and the agents into an elevator, erased the last half-hour's activity from their minds and sent them up to the fourth floor. She then beat a hasty retreat out the door and into Ali's waiting cab.

"Let's get out of here," she suggested. Ali complied.

The town car arrived at the corner by the market shortly after Serena had left with Ali. Naomi didn't wait for the driver to open the door for her. She just slid inside and told the driver to get her over to the Pentagon. When the driver asked for a more specific destination, Naomi simply told her to get her to a manned entrance, preferably as close to the CNO's office as possible.

When they pulled up at a Pentagon entrance, Naomi just said, "Wait for me. I won't be long."

Naomi went up to the door, found it unlocked and went inside. There was a manned guard post about twenty feet away. She went up to it and announced to a rather startled Marine guard, "I need to see the CNO, or his current representative, right now. Please call an appropriate duty officer in grade O-3 or higher."

"You don't want much," the guard sneered. By the time he hit the floor, he had stopped sneering.

"Let's try again," Naomi said as the guard scrambled to his feet. He tried to reach for his gun, but his hand missed his holster and grabbed hold of his crotch instead. "Now get that DO over here on the double," Naomi hissed, "or your fingers are going to get a whole lot tighter."

The guard was a valiant Marine, but he could not fight Naomi. He clumsily called for the duty officer with his left hand. In a few moments, a young Navy commander approached the guard desk.

"Good evening, Commander," Naomi greeted him. "Do you remember a little briefing that was classified Top Secret Cosmic?"

The commander did a double take, first at Naomi's appearance, then at what she represented. "I think I do," he managed to stammer.

"Good," Naomi reassured him, "We need to talk. Is there somewhere less public we can go?"

"This way," the commander said.

As they left the guard desk, Naomi released the Marine from his grasp. "Thank you, Corporal," she purred. Naomi and the commander walked a few yards down a corridor and stopped by a closed office.

"If you remember your briefing," Naomi began, "you will know how important it is not to hinder us when we are on a mission. Are you familiar with the rogue Frigate?"

"How do you know about that?" the astonished commander asked.

"I'll accept that as a ,'yes'," Naomi said. "If you are monitoring the situation in a briefing room, let's go there now. I need to talk to the people who are trying to resolve this issue. I may have some information they don't yet know."

"I can't even get into that area," the commander lamented. "I certainly can't get you in. It's simply impossible."

"Then you had better get me to someone who can get me in," or you are personally going to experience my wrath.

The commander remembered the guard, reluctantly relented and led Naomi through a maze of corridors, stairways and offices to a remote area of the building. There they came to an open vault door beside which was another Marine guard post.

"Is Captain Roberts inside?" the commander asked the guard.

"Yes, Sir" the guard responded.

"Please ask him to come outside," the commander ordered.

In a few minutes Captain Roberts exited the briefing room. He listened to Naomi's situation and escorted her into the briefing room. It was much like the one at San Diego, but somewhat larger. Captain Roberts and Naomi stood at the back of the room.

"Do you know where the Frigate is?" Naomi asked.

"We don't know for sure," the Captain replied. "But we assume it's somewhere just beyond *Cabo San Lucas.* A Mexican patrol boat was destroyed there."

"Is there any way you can stop it?" Naomi queried.

"First, we don't know where it is, second our planes and ships haven't been authorized to go inside Mexican territorial waters," the Captain was frustrated.

"But?" Naomi sensed there was more.

"But we have a sub that's chasing the Frigate," the Captain admitted. "It's still too far away to fire. It's trying to close as fast as possible. It won't be able to fire until it actually gets a permanent fix on the Frigate."

"Okay," Naomi offered, "now it's my turn. From what I have been able to learn, the Frigate's intended target is a spot in the Arizona desert NNE of Tucson. I can't be more specific. Now it's your turn. Tell me about those missiles."

"The Comanche is a medium range missile," the Captain explained. "It comes in a variety of models. According to a copy of their munitions annex sent here from San Diego, the Frigate loaded two thermonuclear missiles. They were supposed to load type-E missiles, but there seems to be some confusion with regard to that. I can't really be more precise than that without knowing exactly what type they have."

"If they were type-E's?" Naomi persisted.

"Cruise range of 300-400 miles," Captain Roberts answered. "Level flight or high arc. Air or ground burst. No loiter capability."

"Can the missiles be aborted once they have been launched.?" It was Naomi's last hope.

"Nope," the Captain replied. "Once they are launched, they can not be diverted or destroyed by command. They will persist to their target. They could be shot down, if you had a super swift rocket or aircraft that could acquire the missile in time to shoot it down. Definitely far from a sure thing. And you would have to have the plane or rocket almost under the missiles track."

"I trust that you will do your best to stop the Frigate," Naomi said solemnly. "There are a lot of innocent lives depending on you." Captain Roberts looked rather curiously at Naomi. "Now," she said. "Can you get someone to show me how to get back to my starting point? I have a car waiting."

As Naomi was leaving the Pentagon, her cell phone rang. It was Serena. "Meet me at Westover Place."

Chapter 14

Homeland Security

Westover Place was in NW Washington, beyond the Naval Observatory. It was a little out of the town car driver's usual neighborhood. It took him a few minutes to locate Ali's cab. As soon as he did, Naomi paid him off and switched vehicles.

Once she was ensconced in Ali's cab with Serena, they compared notes.

"You won't believe this," Serena began. "The person who asked the Director to validate the coordinates was no less than Alan Burke, the Secretary for Homeland Security!"

Naomi did a double tale at that news. "You mean," she exclaimed, "after he saw what we did to his boss, he wanted to take us on again?"

"More like he wanted to get even," Serena replied. "How are we going to handle this?"

"Do we know where he lives?" Naomi asked. "We don't have much time. And I'm going to be in a really nasty mood if we have to do this after the Valley has been destroyed."

"Pardon me for interfering," Ali suddenly interrupted, "but maybe I can help."

Naomi and Serena looked up quite startled. They had entirely forgotten that Ali was sitting in the front seat of the cab.

"How can you help, Ali?" Serena asked.

"Well," Ali said, "I and my friends have picked up and dropped off most folks who live in the District. Most of the VIP's only get limo and town car service on official business. We handle the after hours trade. Want me to check out this Alan Burke character?"

"Ali, you a re a jewel," Naomi said. "See what you can find, but not a word as to why. Understand?"

"You bet!" Ali said and started making radio calls. It took over fifteen minutes, but he finally hit pay dirt.

"I've got an address over in Spring Valley; it's just a few miles away. Shall we go?"

"How did you get this info, Ali?" Naomi asked. "It would definitely not be good for us to barge in at the wrong address."

Driver picked up him and the Misses the other night and took them to a concert," Ali responded. "He paid with a credit card and the driver had to validate it before he could accept it. No doubt about the address."

"Then, let's go, Ali," Serena said. "We have no time to waste."

In fifteen minutes, Ali's cab was sitting at the curb next door to Burke's house. Naomi and Serena checked out their target, looking for guards, spotlights, traps or alarms. There was nothing obvious, so Serena started looking for active circuits. She found three in front and disabled them. Naomi looked for an active brain. Finding none, she looked for a dog. Still nothing.

"Okay," Naomi declared. "We're clear. Ali, wait for us." Then they were off.

A quick sprint across the lawn took them to the front door. Serena cracked the locks and the security system. They were inside. Naomi guided them to the appropriate upstairs bedroom. She was about to turn the knob, when Serena suddenly pulled her back.

"Alarm," Serena whispered. Then she paused, probing gently.

"Sonic," Serena whispered. "I have to find a passive receptor." She continued searching. Naomi knew that Serena did good work, but she was becoming antsy. She waited nervously in the dark, anxiously searching for any unwanted presence.

"Trap!" Serena whispered. "There are two receptors! Just about got it. Okay! We're clear."

Serena silently opened the bedroom door. The room was dark, but, by now, both their eyes had accommodated to the darkness. The ambient light from a window provided sufficient illumination to make out the arrangement of the room. There was a chest and bath to the left. A double dresser sat to the right along with a large walk-in closet. Opposite the door was a king-size bed with two bodies sleeping soundly.

Naomi immobilized the female on the left and ensured that she would continue sleeping. Then she went up to the right side of the bed and said, in a loud demanding voice, "Get your lousy rump out of that bed and come with us. You've got a lot of explaining to do!"

Alan Burke jerked himself awake in half a heartbeat and sat bolt upright in the bed. He quickly looked around and took in the two Elders. Somehow he had been found out. Well, he had half expected this. He even tried to smile. He was about to accomplish his goal of destroying those blasted aliens. In the future the world would consider him a martyr,

Naomi interrupted his reverie. "How did you convince the captain of the Frigate to undertake this stupid mission?" she asked.

"Captain Richard Burke is my son. The orders were perfect forgeries," Burke answered, "It wasn't difficult."

"What exactly are his orders?" Serena posed.

"To load included guidance chips into the missiles, proceed to a certain point, launch the missiles." Burke responded.

"And if he is stopped?" Naomi asked.

"To fire the missiles, regardless of location."

"Is there any recall code, any way he can be stopped?" Serena was almost begging.

"No," was the short answer. Then Burke evidently felt the need to share his intelligent plan.

"My son thinks this is just a fox and hounds exercise. That his missiles have dummy warheads on them. If he is following the plan, he will have disabled his radios and be depending solely on radar and sonar. Should he be trapped, he is to fire the missiles and surrender. If he gets to the designated position, he is to fire his missiles and attempt to escape. He will surrender whenever he is trapped.

"Whatever happens, my son gets off Scot free. He was only following what he thought were official Navy orders. If there is any blame assigned, it will fall on me. I didn't really expect to get away with this. My only hope is that eventually the people will thank me for ridding this planet of the alien menace. What few are left over can easily be rounded up and disposed of."

"And what about the Mexican Navy patrol boat he destroyed? Naomi asked. "Is that just insignificant collateral damage?"

"What patrol boat?" Burke was astounded. "He had no authority to do that."

"Maybe your son felt that he was given that ammunition and those torpedoes for a reason." Naomi chided.

"At any rate," Serena added, "Your son will be brought up on charges of high treason, piracy, murder, and incidental theft of government property among a host of other charges. He will either get the death penalty from the US or Mexico or spend the rest of his life in prison at hard labor."

"And," Naomi said quietly, "you will not be around to appreciate your personal acclamation or your son's demise. You are about to experience eternal damnation."

With that, Naomi caused Burke to lie back down in bed. In a few seconds, he was blind, deaf, dumb and paralyzed. Most of his nervous system was shut down, permanently. Naomi gently lifted her hold on Mrs. Burke.

Then Naomi and Serena retraced their steps, reestablishing the various alarm systems as they went. They dashed quickly back across the lawn to Ali's waiting cab. The sun was just creeping up over the eastern horizon.

As Ali pulled up to the market in the Elders neighborhood, Serena leaned forward and whispered in Ali's ear, "You have been privy to entirely too much information tonight, Ali. I strongly suggest that you forget all of it."

At the same time Naomi made sure that the events of the night were permanently erased from Ali's mind.

Ali just shook his head and wondered at the three crisp hundred dollar bills that had materialized in his shirt pocket. He looked around, but the cab and the street were empty. 'Those two again,' he mused, with a slight smile.

When they got back to their apartment, Naomi sat down at the computer.

"I'm going to send an update to the Valley," she said as Serena plopped down on the couch.

"What can we tell them except that the perpetrator is taken care of?" Serena asked.

"Something about that missile still bothers me," Naomi explained. "Getting information out of that Captain at the Pentagon about the missiles was like pulling hen's teeth. In the first place he wasn't sure what kind of missile the Frigate took on board. Secondly, I got the impression there was a significant difference between two types of missiles, and he wouldn't discuss the difference. I want to strongly suggest that they follow up on this situation."

Chapter 15

Launch

Captain Burke had been driving the Frigate north through the center of the Gulf of California at full power. The submarine that he had picked up at Cabo was still following. So far, he had been able to stay ahead of it. Never allowing the sub captain to get a firing solution on him. Now, the end was in sight, in more ways that one.

"Chief," Burke called out, "get up here."

About two seconds later, the Chief emerged from the CIC, "Aye, Sir … "

"We're getting close to Guaymas, Chief," the Captain reported. "there is a highway close to the shore there. I'm going to pull in close to the shore so you and the crew can abandon ship. You can follow the highway north to the town. Last thing before you go, link the CIC and engineering to the bridge. According to the specs, one person is supposed to be able to run the ship from here in an emergency. Go below and get the crew ready to go. We have about fifteen minutes. And ask Lt. Baker to join me on the Bridge."

"Aye, Sir," the Chief responded and disappeared down into the CIC.

A few minutes later Jeff Baker emerged from the CIC.

"The Chief told me what's going on," he said. "What do you want me to do?"

"I want you to take charge of the men and get them safely back to the US," Captain Burke responded. "When you get back, blame me for everything. I commandeered the Frigate. I took out the Mexican patrol boat. I am solely responsible for everything. Neither you nor the crew played any part in our activities. You've been a good Exec, Baker. I wish we could have served in more peaceful times. You'd better prepare to abandon ship."

Lt. Baker silently saluted the Captain and went back down below decks. There was nothing else to be said.

Captain Burke steered the Frigate in toward the shore. He began to slow about 900 yards out, and, when he had closed to within 300 yards he retracted the hydrofoil and changed to silent running. He found a nice little cove and eased the little ship into it and came to a stop.

"Captain to crew," he barked over the ship's communicator, "Now hear this! Abandon Ship! I repeat. Abandon ship!" Burke watched as Lt Baker, the Chief and the rest of the crew dropped overboard and waded ashore. When they were well clear of the Frigate, Burke increased power and steered back into the main channel. He increased the power further and dropped the hydrofoil.

As soon as he was making maximum speed up the Gulf, Burke checked the sonar and radar displays. There was a slow-moving aircraft over the Pacific shadowing the Frigate just outside the twelve-mile limit. The sub was closer, but still not close enough to shoot. If he could keep up this speed he would be able to launch in about three hours.

Burke had charted his course well. Ahead in the Gulf were a group of islands that almost completely blocked the channel. The Frigate would be able to navigate through them, but the sub couldn't get through. The channel was too narrow and too shallow to let it continue through submerged.

Burke had already concluded that the US had still not yet received permission to enter Mexican waters. The only way the sub could have followed him so far was submerged. If it surfaced it could be spotted and probably cause a serious international incident.

There was a small channel between the western coast and the islands which was designed to permit shipping and fishing boats to pass through the area. If the sub chose that path, it would be unable to turn around. To reverse course, it would either have to back out – a risky and slow process. Or, it would have to continue all the way through and then turn around in the northern end of the Gulf. That area was so shallow that sub might even be forced to surface there.

All Burke had to do was make it to the islands. He double checked the missiles. They were both armed. He flipped the switch covers open and set the switches to the 'Ready' position. His fingers were twitching. He started to wipe the sweat from his brow. His hands were shaking.

Burke had never been in combat before. He didn't quite know what to expect. He would find out as the hours and minutes passed. Time was either eternally slow or fantastically fast. 'Why couldn't it just move smoothly?' he wondered.

The sub captain was keeping close track of the Frigate. The plane crew had noted the deviation in movement when the Frigate went in toward the coast, but they didn't know why. They couldn't see the crew abandoning the ship.

The sub was only allowed to listen to the aircraft's reports. It could not break radio silence. That would give away their existence to anyone who might be listening. Of course, they assumed the Frigate knew they were following, but that was intended to be more intimidating than fatal. Still, the torpedoes were loaded in their tubes, ready to be used if the need should arise.

The sub captain had also studied the layout of the Gulf. He knew what lay ahead. He was not happy about it. He had his orders: stop the Frigate. Use any method at hand.

"Clark," the Captain called on his Exec, "Why haven't we got a firing solution on that Frigate, yet?

"His course is too erratic, Captain" the Exec answered. He's too far away still to get a lock on him long enough to get a fish to him."

"Compute probable time to lock." The Captain ordered. The Exec started punching numbers into a calculator. In a few minutes he had an answer.

"If the Frigate stays on its present course," Captain, "we may be able to get a shooting solution on it just as it gets to the islands. It will be touch and go, though."

"Work up a few scenarios, so we'll have something to work with," the Captain directed. "We may not have much time."

Captain Burke was feeling the stress of his mission. He was tired and nervous. He had only one thought in mind, get past the islands and launch the missiles. After that he could just run the Frigate aground on one of the islands and get some rest.

Just to lie down and rest for a few minutes – it sounded so inviting. Suddenly he jerked awake. He had just fallen asleep on his feet. He needed some coffee; but he couldn't leave the bridge long enough to go get it.

Burke opened the Captain's log and made a note. 'Provide coffee for the bridge on critical missions'. Of course, that was silly. He was suppose to have a crew, any one of which would be able to provide a cup of coffee – if they were still on board.

He was nearing the first islands. There were two large islands, one on either side of the Gulf. These were separated by a small archipelago that spread between them. Burke was aiming for a small gap between two of the islands in the archipelago.

He slowed the Frigate and drew up the hydroplane. The sub was now closing rapidly. Then the sub stopped abruptly. Burke watched, fascinated as the sub slowly turned and began to leave the area at high speed.

Burke had to switch his attention back to his own course. He was quickly approaching the first islands. When he had adjusted his course, he looked at the radar screen. The aircraft was also leaving the area. This was upsetting. Burke searched his screens for a new threat. There was none. A few small fishing boats ahead, but no threat.

Burke picked up speed and cleared the island chain. He was soon free and clear in the northern Gulf. He reached out to the missile launch buttons. His hand hesitated over the switches. Burke noted that he was no longer nervous. His mind was crystal clear. His nerves steady. It was time to execute his mission. His fingers rested on the two launch buttons momentarily. Then he pressed them simultaneously.

The Frigate jerked and shuddered as the two missiles roared into action and leapt out of their launch tubes. In a few seconds they were streaking up into the sky on their way to their targets.

Commander Burke brought the Frigate to a full stop. He had accomplished his mission. Perhaps the sub had retreated in recognition of that fact. The game was now over. He made his way down to his cabin and collapsed onto his bunk. He really needed the sleep that quickly overwhelmed him.

Chapter 16

Terrorists!

When Tom Watson got back to Tucson, the Admirals plane had been refueled and was ready to return to San Diego. He called the duty officer at the office and told him to pick up the station vehicle on Monday. Tom was returning to San Diego, ostensibly to pick up his car. He said he would be back in the office on Tuesday.

The flight back was uneventful. Tom took advantage of the flight to get some sleep. He was awakened just as they touched down at the Air/Sea Rescue airport. No sooner had he stepped off the plane than his cell phone went off. Sheriff Billy Eagle was on the line. He wanted to pass on the information from Naomi and Serena.

By the time Tom hung up the call, his purpose in San Diego had completely changed. He jumped into his car and made a mad dash for the COMPACWEST headquarters, breaking several base speed limits on the way.

He parked on the side of the building and rushed inside, fumbling for his pass on the way. He waved the pass at the guard as he passed and headed down the stairs to the Command Briefing Room. There was a new guard on the door, who didn't recognize Tom from his previous visit.

"Pass and ID", the guard demanded.

Tom fumbled through his pockets and finally found everything. The guard scanned them, looked at his list of authorized visitors – and didn't find Tom's name listed.

"I'm Sorry, Sir," the guard said, "but I don't see your name on the authorized personnel list. Is there someone I can call?"

Tom still needed sleep. He was tired, anxious and frustrated. Now he was adding mad to the list. "You're damn right there is!" Tom asserted. "Just ask Admiral Lewis to step out here, if you have the *cojones*!"

The guard hesitated a moment too long. Tom was on his case. He pulled out his cell phone and waved it in the guard's direction. "Look!" Tom insisted. "Call the Admiral, or open the door, or I'll call the Admiral!" Another wave of the cell phone. "And, if I call him, he is not going to be pleased with your performance!"

It took the guard half a second to get the big picture. He quickly handed Tom back his ID and pressed the button to open the door. "Sorry, Sir, we have to be careful about terrorists," the guard mumbled as Tom slipped quietly inside.

The room was much as he left it. A new Captain was chairing the meeting in place of the Admiral. Fred was still there as were most of the earlier participants. The display screen showed the lower portion of the Baja Peninsula. There were several blips in the Pacific west of the peninsula. One of them was bright green, the others were blue. There was a blue blip just outside the Gulf moving north.

Tom sat down beside Fred who looked up in surprise. "Anything new?" Tom whispered.

"They now have a command structure in place," Fred whispered back. "That green blip in the Pacific is a Navy patrol plane, codename 'Hound dog. We are in constant communication with it. It is tracking the Frigate as it moves north in the Gulf. It, in turn, is broadcasting any changes to the sub that's about to enter the Gulf. The sub is running silent, so the Mexicans won't know she's there.

"Otherwise, nothing new and no idea what is going on."

"Well," Tom said, somewhat louder, "I have some news."

As Tom hoped, his comment got the Captain's attention.

"And who are you?" the Captain inquired, looking in Tom's direction.

"Special Agent Tom Watson, Tucson Station Chief," Tom Began. "Fred and I" with a brief nod toward Fed Winston, "were here for the Frigate's commissioning and just sort of stayed on. At least Fred did, I have been out doing a little intelligence gathering, with a kind assist from Admiral Lewis."

"And just what kind of 'intelligence' did you acquire?" the Captain asked with a not too small sense of disdain.

"I have confirmed," Tom explained calmly, "that the Frigate's target is a spot in the Arizona desert, not too far from Tucson. I have also learned that the source of this little exercise was Secretary Burke of Homeland Security. He has been dealt with. I have also been told that the solution to the current problem involves determining the exact difference between the Type-E and Type-J Comanches."

"We've already talked to the Officer in Charge of the Arsenal," the Captain replied. "He told us that the Type-J is just the same as the Type-E, but the Type-J has an improved navigation system."

"How improved?" Tom shot back. "I told the Admiral about the navigation system yesterday. Isn't there better information available somewhere in this country's Navy?"

"Don't get impertinent, young man," the Captain erupted, or, Special Agent or no, I'll kick you off this base faster than you can blink."

"I'm just trying to help you," Tom pointed out. "The least you could do is try to cooperate. Otherwise, I have a sneaky feeling that your little incident is going to explode all over the map."

"I'm sorry," the Captain apologized. "I guess I'm a little on edge. Not enough sleep and too much coffee."

"Apology accepted," Tom said. "Now doesn't the Navy have a weapons office somewhere that may be able to answer the question. You don't have to tell them why we want to know."

"Yes, we do," a Lt commander on the far side of the table intervened. "The Type-J is a recent development. Before being deployed, it would have been tested at China Lake. They should have all of the specs."

"Of course they will," the Captain agreed. He ordered the Yeoman to connect him to China Lake. Before the call could be placed, the Lt Commander suggested that the call be placed over a secure line, just to save time.

"It took a few minutes to raise the duty officer at the China Lake Naval Weapons Testing Center. He could not answer the question, but he new which office could. He could not transfer the secure phone. He gave the yeoman the number to call and hung up.

The Yeoman tried the new number. It rang for several minutes before someone answered. The Yeoman nodded to the Captain.

"This is Captain Stuart speaking for COMPACWEST," the Captain announced. "we have a situation here and we need to know the exact difference between the Type-E and Type-J Comanche missiles. We understand the missile was recently tested out there. Can you help us?"

That question was followed by a long conversation involving several pauses and a few indecipherable grunts from the Captain. Everyone waited expectantly. Fred, apparently frustrated by typical military bureaucracy, got up and went to the sideboard for a sandwich and a soda.

Finally, the Captain thanked China Lake for the help and hung up the phone. He just sat there in silence for several minutes. Tom watched him carefully. The information had to be unimaginably bad.

Fred couldn't stand it any longer, "Did you get the answer, Captain?"

"I did," the Captain replied. "But, before I tell you what it is, I want to get the Admiral over here. Yeoman, call Admiral Lewis and ask him to come here as soon as possible. In the meantime, gentlemen, I suggest you emulate our good Special Agent and avail yourselves of the refreshments."

Admiral Lewis wasted no time in getting to the Information Center. Everyone stood as he entered the room and Captain Stuart relinquished the seat at the head of the table.

Once the Admiral was seated, he looked over at the Captain and said, "Well, what's up?"

The Captain replied, "Admiral, I have some highly classified weapons data that I secured in regard to the difference between the Type-E and Type-J Comanches. Special Agent Watson suggested that this data might be the solution to our Frigate situation. I agree that it does impact the situation, but, considering the sensitivity of the information, I wanted your permission to release it."

The Admiral paused a moment to digest what the Captain had said. "I think," he said at last, "that the people here have all been privy to some pretty sensitive data so far. Adding a little more is not likely to cause a meltdown of Naval intelligence.

"And to those of you sitting, and standing, around the table," the Admiral added, "what you have heard in this room, or what you may hear, is to remain in this room forever. It is not to be repeated outside this room to anyone for any reason. The penalty for violating my order will be very severe.

"Now, Captain, suppose you tell us what you learned."

Before the Captain could utter a word, the radio suddenly came to life. Hound Dog was reporting that Puppy had made a strange maneuver. The Frigate had moved into the west coast of Mexico for a short period then moved on, somewhat erratically to the island archipelago and was proceeding to pass through them. It would soon be protected from the sub.

The display screen reflected what Hound Dog had said. All could appreciate the new situation. Once safe from the sub, the Frigate would be in position to launch.

"Captain, I think we need that information," the Admiral said.

"I spoke with the Director of Test Operations at China Lake," the Captain said. "He told me that the Type-J was modified to prevent it from ever being used by terrorists to attack the United States. If a Comanche ever crosses the United States' border inbound, the navigation system will immediately swap the destination and source coordinates and change course accordingly."

"You mean," the Admiral asked incredulously, "that, if the Frigate launches its missiles into Arizona from the Gulf of Mexico, they will turn around and strike the Frigate."

The Captain simply said, "Yes."

The Admiral grabbed the radio microphone, "Doghouse to Hound Dog," he practically screamed. As soon as Hound Dog acknowledged the call, the Admiral said, "Hound Dog, tell your puppy to turn around immediately and get the heck out of the Gulf. Then you change course due west and put a hundred miles between you and Mexico. Tell puppy to resume normal operations and you return to base. Exercise Fox and Hounds is suspended as of now. Do you copy?"

As soon as the message had been acknowledged as understood, the Admiral signed off.

"There's no reason to persist in stopping the Frigate," the Admiral admitted. "We could never get to it in time. I think I had better notify the Secretary of State that we are about to have a little problem with Mexico."

"What if the Frigate Captain found a way to disable the navigation system?" the Lt Commander asked.

"The course-reversal circuitry was integral to the navigation system," the Captain explained. "It could not be disabled by itself. And the Comanche can not be fired without an operational navigation system."

At that moment, the display screen announced an inbound missile. A pair of tracks appeared leading from the Gulf of Mexico toward Arizona. Everyone at the table stared in silence. When the tracks crossed the US border, there was a little hiccough and the tracks continued back across the border toward the Gulf. A few seconds, later the display announced a pair of nuclear explosions in the Gulf.

"Well," Tom announced as he rose from his seat, "I guess it's high time I got back to Tucson. I'll be in touch, Fred." Fred nodded in reply.

Tom walked slowly out of the headquarters building to where his Mustang was parked. He drove well within the speed limit off the base and back to Interstate 8. When he was on the Interstate headed to Arizona, he floored it. It was good to put San Diego, the Navy and the Frigate far behind him.

Epilogue

Red Hawk paused. She closed her eyes and rested for a few minutes. Then she looked up and continued, "As you know the Elders have had no further problems with Homeland Security or any other government agency. I do not foresee any problems in your future.

"At first, Mexico was highly miffed at two nuclear explosions on their territory. But, when they had actually inspected the site and determined that no real harm had been done, they relented and settled for a large remunerations payment and a promise from us not to do it again.

"The Frigate's crew initially made their way toward Guaymas. One of the crewmen thought he saw the missile track as it left the Frigate. But when there was an explosion in the vicinity of the Frigate, they assumed that one or both of the missiles had malfunctioned.

"At any rate, the crew made its way slowly to Hermosillo and up to the border at Yuma. Nogales would have been closer, but they still didn't know what exactly had happened and decided to avoid central and eastern Arizona. They turned themselves in at the Marine Corps detachment at the Yuma Airport.

"The Crew was flown back to San Diego and interrogated at length. They convinced the top brass that they really had nothing to do with the planned attack and they were eventually released to continue their military careers with no blemish on their records.

"The Frigate itself was totally destroyed in the nuclear blasts from the returning missiles. It was assumed that Commander Burke had been killed by the blasts. No evidence has yet arisen to dispute that hypothesis.

"Apparently, Special Agent Tom Watson did not tell anyone about his encounters with the Elders. The next time you venture into the Council chambers, you will see a new plaque hanging on the wall of the common area. It honors Tom Watson as an official human friend of the Elder people.

"I am sorry to announce that Special Agent Tom Watson was recently killed in the line of duty. He and a fellow agent had tracked a notorious Mexican drug lord to an abandoned warehouse in Tucson. In an ensuing gun battle, Tom tried to lure the drug lord out into the open and was shot and killed in the process. His effort gave his partner a clear shot and the drug lord was also killed."

Red Hawk slowly closed her eyes, indicating the lesson was over. Then, with the help of her totem stick, she rose and walked slowly to the cave. She and White Wolf left the valley.

== 30 ==

Also by Robyn Kelly:

The Elder Chronicles: The Lost World

The Elder Chronicles: Birth of a Savior

The Elder Chronicles: Elder Child

The Elder Chronicles: The Legend of Red Hawk

The Elder Chronicles: Elder Escape

The Elder Chronicles: New Breed

The Elder Chronicles: Elena's Plan

The Elder Chronicles: Mutation

Watch for volume ten

The Elder Chronicles: Elder Reunion

Coming Soon!